DEATH OR GLORY BOYS

Theresa Breslin

EGMONT

'Reconciliation' by Siegfried Sassoon is reproduced
by permission of George Sassoon.

First published in Great Britain 1996
by Methuen Books Ltd
This edition published 2002
by Egmont Books Limited
239 Kensington High Street
London W8 6SA

Text copyright © 1996 Theresa Breslin
Cover illustration copyright © 2002 Darren Hopes

The moral rights of the author and the cover illustrator
have been asserted

ISBN 1 4052 0109 6

10 9 8 7 6 5 4 3 2 1

A CIP catalogue record for this title
is available from the British Library

Typeset by Avon DataSet Ltd,
Bidford on Avon, Warwickshire B50 4JH
Printed and bound in Great Britain
by Cox & Wyman Ltd, Reading, Berkshire

For my soldier, soldier

Contents

Contents

1 Cal

Cal, glancing at watch, working slowly, was aware that there was not much time. But . . . couldn't hurry this part of it, dangerous to rush now, when everything else had run along so smoothly.

Very smoothly.

An assured walk past the desk to the back of the shop, a brief authoritative nod at the young girl coming from her teabreak in the staffroom, and then on down the access stairs to the basement stockrooms.

So easy.

But then the British respected authority, obeyed commands.

Obedient.

Stupid.

1

Cal grimaced as the fuse slid to one side.

'Slow down boy, slow down,' whispered quietly.

Better like this anyway. Always leave it that there was never enough time. No time to think then. No time to wonder. How it might feel. To be there when it went off. Caught in the flames – because it would burn, and very rapidly. Aisle upon aisle of shoes, boots, slippers. Shining leather, man-made fibre, soft infills. The packaging, the cardboard boxes, the tissue paper, all catching fire swiftly.

Unstoppable.

Looking around, anyone caught here would die. Incinerated in seconds. And just above . . . clustered round the sales desk. There wouldn't be a bell to sound a warning. Fire alarm already disconnected. No point in doing it at all if not done properly. Modern technology – so simple to dismantle. Basic electronic knowledge could immobilise the fire system. Easy enough for a child to do it.

Fingers falter. Thinking of a child. The child that might be in the shop above, having shoes bought. New shoes. Push that thought away. Down. Quickly below the surface. They deserved it. There . . . now it was gone, with all the other sentiment.

Glancing at watch. Time I wasn't here. Get up. Slide the box with its deadly contents back among the old stock.

Walk casually back. Breathe slowly. Cheek, that was necessary . . . and flair. Pause, friendly smile at the girl on the till. Yes, definitely flair.

Cal glanced in the shop window on leaving, spoke aloud. 'Must buy myself a heavy jacket and a pair of boots before winter sets in.'

'Boots,' said Sarah Bell as they turned out of the school gate. She linked her arm through her friend Maggie's. 'My mission this afternoon is to buy myself a pair of boots. I've spent the last three weeks saving baby-sitting money and culling cash from the parents, and I'm not going home without them tonight.'

'Are you coming with us?' Maggie called back to the two boys who were walking along the road behind them. 'We're on a mission. Boots for Bell.'

Phil, the taller and darker of the two, looked at David and raised one eyebrow. 'What d'you reckon? Could we survive a shopping expedition with the gruesome twosome?'

David shrugged. 'An hour to spare before rugby practice. Why not?' They increased their pace to catch up with the girls. 'It wouldn't be rugby boots you're looking for?' said David. 'In my size so that I could borrow them occasionally?'

'Fat chance,' laughed Sarah.

'Let's try in here,' said Maggie, pushing open the shoe shop door on the Main Street and dragging Sarah inside. 'Come along you two.' She held the door open for David and Phil.

'Which colour?' asked David once they were inside.

'Black,' said Sarah.

David went to the nearest display stand and picked up a pair of black boots. 'Here,' he said, 'try these.'

Sarah barely glanced at them. 'Oh, I don't know. Let's see what else there is.'

'What's wrong with them?' asked David. He turned and held them out to Maggie. 'What's wrong with these?'

'You are joking, aren't you? I mean, you don't actually expect her to buy the first thing she sees, do you?' Maggie grimaced at Sarah. 'Boys are useless to take shopping,' she said. 'Absolutely useless.' The two girls wandered off to the other side of the store.

'Sarah, what kind of boots are you looking for exactly?' said Phil, following after them.

'She doesn't know *exactly*,' said Maggie. 'Obviously nobody knows *exactly* what it is they're looking for until they find it.'

David made circling motions with his forefinger at the side of his head. 'Nuts,' he said to Phil. 'Women in shops are nuts.' He gazed about him for a moment or two. Then his

4

eye caught that of a blonde assistant lounging by the till. 'With maybe a few exceptions,' he added. 'Here mate hold that,' he shoved his rucksack at Phil and, smoothing back his hair, he went across to the sales desk.

'Oh for heaven's sake look at him,' said Maggie. 'Casanova McCall. Any opportunity and he's off.'

'Long boots? Ankle boots? Laced? Heeled? Zipped? What?' persisted Phil.

Maggie had stopped to examine the new-range stand.

'Ummm, kind of chunky, I think,' said Sarah. 'Yes, chunky, and long, probably, but definitely black.'

Maggie picked up a shoe in rose-coloured suede. 'Sarah, look at these!' she exclaimed.

'Perfect!' said Sarah. 'Absolutely perfect! I must try them.' She slipped one on. 'These would go exactly with that dress in Top Shop that I want for Christmas.'

Phil came up behind her. 'Boots,' he said in her ear. 'Concentrate girl. Boots. Do you intend to buy boots today? Do you intend to buy boots at all?'

'Of course I intend to buy boots,' said Sarah. 'That's what we came into the shop for. Chunky boots.'

'May I enquire, then,' said Phil folding his arms, 'if you are on a mission to purchase long, chunky, black boots, why you are, in fact, at this very moment trying on a flat pink shoe?'

Maggie and Sarah looked at him and then at each other. 'See what I mean?' said Maggie. 'As shoppers, men are hopeless.'

'Do they have any uses at all?' enquired Sarah. She picked up a matching handbag and swung the shoulder strap across her arm. 'What do you think?'

Phil ran his fingers through his hair. 'Why,' he asked with exaggerated patience, 'have you now put on that handbag?'

Sarah stared at him. 'Because it matches the shoes,' she said gently. She stretched up and patted him on the head. 'Ask your mummy to explain it to you when you get home tonight.'

Phil reached out quickly and grabbed her hand. 'We could go for a coffee and *you* could explain it to me, very slowly.'

'Emm . . . I have to go home quite soon. I said I would start the dinner tonight. It was part of the deal for the boots.' Sarah looked at his hand. 'Can I have my hand back now?'

Phil released her hand, finger by finger, and Sarah felt her face go warm. She turned to find that Maggie was intently studying the remaining handbags.

'There you are!' said Maggie, with exaggerated surprise. She gave Sarah a secret nudge. 'Told you,' she hissed.

Sarah shook her head slightly, but she knew what

Maggie meant. Over the last few weeks Phil had taken to joining their group at school breaktime, and Maggie had already decided that he was waiting for an opportunity to ask Sarah out.

'Ice rink, Pyramid Centre, Saturday night,' said David suddenly reappearing beside them. He nudged Phil. 'Her name's Kirsty and she's bringing a pal for you.'

Phil glared at him. 'I don't want her pal.' He glanced at Sarah. 'I've told you before to leave me out of your dating arrangements.'

David looked from one to the other. 'Ah, right, right,' he said quickly. 'I meant everybody, of course. All of us that is.' He pulled Maggie by the arm. 'Maggie's coming, aren't you?' He gave her an imploring look. 'And you're bringing Sarah? We'll all go together.'

'David, my lad,' said Maggie, 'you are a seriously sad person, and will have to be taken in hand. Bromide in your tea, or whatever Mr Eliott our esteemed English teacher told us they fed to the soldiers in the First World War to lower their sex drive. I recommend you swallow a bucket of it. This is a shoe shop, not Dave's Dating Agency. We came in here to buy boots, remember?'

'Exactly,' said David smugly, 'and my friend Kirsty said she had new styles in and she is bringing them across right now.'

'Oh good,' said Phil. He sat down on a stool. 'I hope they are kind of chunky, probably long, and definitely black.' He opened his rucksack and took out a poetry book. 'This talk of Mr Eliott reminds me we've work to hand in to him tomorrow. I'm going to have a small helping of Rupert Brooke while you lot find madam a pair of boots.'

'This always happens to me,' complained Sarah twenty minutes later. 'I find the perfect boots and they don't have my size.'

'Do you ever go up to Crosston at all?' asked Kirsty.

'Well my aunt stays just outside,' said Sarah. 'Why?'

'We've a branch in the big shopping centre there. Do you want me to phone and see if they've got these in your size, and then your aunt could pick them up for you?'

'Great,' said Sarah, 'thanks very much.'

'Hang on then,' said Kirsty. She gave David a huge smile. 'I'll ask my manageress if I can make the call for you.'

Six call boxes. Every one of them out of order. They didn't deserve a warning. Cal clenched the wheel, hands trembling. Now that was bad. In this line of work, shaky hands you don't need. Staring at them, willing them to stop. Deep breaths. Why so upset? Take a moment . . . yes. It had been the thought of the child buying shoes . . . own memories with Mamma. Close eyes for a moment and lean

8

back. Then . . . eyes open now, hands still again. Smile. That's the way. There would be no warning. Too bad.

Had to get away, well clear of any road blocks. No, wait. There. A call box at the end of that road. One last try. Pull over . . .

'Blast!'

Someone in it. Two youths . . . finishing up, leaving the booth.

Switch off the ignition, take some change, get out of the car . . .

One boy noticing, turned back, gave the two fingers, then grabbed the receiver and violently wrenched it from the wall.

Cal stopped, angry. Then smiled. Tough luck. Hope one of your mates is in that shoe shop.

Looked at the time on the dashboard clock.

Right now in fact.

'It's ringing,' said Kirsty to Sarah, 'though they always take ages to answer – Oh hi! Susan, it's me, Kirsty at Longheath,' she paused. 'Yeah, fine, fine. Listen, could you check if you've got these boots in a five?' She flicked her fringe out of her eyes and grinned at David. 'Yeah,' she went on, 'I'll give you the code number.' She picked up the box and looked at the end panel. Then she frowned. 'Eh, Susan?' she said. 'Susan? What was *that*?' She laughed into the mouthpiece. 'Hey what are you lot doing? Sounds like a wild party.' She stopped suddenly and her face changed colour and then she thrust the receiver at the shop manageress. 'Something bad's happening up there,' she stuttered.

The manageress took the phone and suddenly the little group gathered round the sales desk could hear what Kirsty had heard: on the other end of the line someone was screaming.

2 Incident one – Crosston

The shop manageress held the receiver away from her. The screaming became hysterical sobs. She looked at them wide-eyed. 'I'll have to hang up and cut her off,' she whispered, 'or I won't be able to phone the police.'

It was Phil who moved first. 'I'll go next door to the baker's shop and get them to call the emergency services,' he said. He dropped his rucksack and ran.

There was a silence in the shop. It was more frightening than the noise had been. The line had gone dead. The manageress replaced the telephone on its cradle and stared at it for a moment or two. Then she said, 'I'll phone our head office. Someone there should be told.' She picked up the phone, put it back down and managed a half-smile at Sarah, David and Maggie. 'Look, I think you should go home. I'm sorry, but there's nothing you can do here. Just give me a note of your names and addresses in case I need to get in touch.' She gave them paper and a pen, then looked at the girl standing beside her. 'I need to see to my staff. Kirsty, go and take a teabreak. Now,' she added, and pushed Kirsty gently in the direction of the staffroom.

They met Phil outside the baker's. Sarah handed him his rucksack.

'You OK?' he asked her.

She shook her head. 'I don't know. What do you think was going on?'

Phil shrugged. 'Maybe she had a really awkward customer. Like you,' he added.

Sarah punched him on the arm. 'You've got fast reactions.' She flicked at the cover of the poetry book which he still held in his hand. 'Pretty quick thinking for someone who is into poetry in a serious way.'

'That's a stereotypical remark,' said Phil reprovingly. 'It doesn't follow that, just because I like poems, I am not a macho-man.' His eyes gleamed. 'Come and watch me play rugby.' He stood on tiptoe and leaned over her menacingly. 'I can get quite physical, you know.'

Again Sarah felt her face colour. 'Another time,' she said lightly. She lowered her gaze from his.

'What is it with you and poetry anyway, Phil?' said

Maggie. 'You practically pounced on that last English assignment just because Eliott said we would have to look at a few rhymes.'

'A few rhymes!' said Phil. 'A few rhymes! You ignorant child. We are studying the War Poets in case you hadn't noticed. They composed some of the most moving, majestic and tragic verse ever written.' He lifted his book and smacked her smartly on top of the head.

'Oww!' She grabbed the book from him. 'Rupert Brooke,' she said. 'Well he has certainly made an impression on me, even if it's only a large dent on my head.' She opened a page. 'Here, look at this photograph, Sarah. He was a bit of a babe, was Rupert.'

Sarah studied the face of the good-looking young man, chin resting on his left hand, who gazed out at her. 'Mmmm . . . don't know. He looks a bit too deep for me.' She glanced sideways at Phil and then smiled at Maggie. 'You know these poetic types, you can never trust them.'

'Well it says here in the book that he was gorgeous,' said Maggie. 'He was called "A young Apollo, golden-haired". He had stunning blue eyes and everybody fancied him rotten.'

Phil leaned over Maggie's shoulder. 'Pity my hair is dark and my eyes are brown,' he said. 'But never mind,

Sarah prefers macho-men. She just told me that, didn't you Sarah?' He stared straight at her.

Sarah put her head on one side and stared back at him. 'Actually I didn't,' she said. 'I said you had fast reactions.'

'Yeah, I'd say he was pretty fast,' said David. 'People get completely the wrong idea about my pal Phil. Teachers think he's the perfect gentleman, studious and well mannered. Girls think he's Boy Wonder, whereas I know he's a boy racer. *I* am the one who gets the bad press. My reputation seems to be that all my time is spent chasing members of the opposite sex. Incidentally,' he took the poetry book from Maggie's hand, 'are there any pictures in here of *female* war poets? My enquiry is, of course, purely for academic research.'

'Aren't we supposed to be studying the poetry rather than the poets?' said Sarah.

'Well there's a thing,' said Maggie. 'It may, in fact, be boringly true that Mr Eliott did intend us to absorb some literature at some point in our last year at school.'

'You know,' said David, handing the book back to Phil. 'You could save us all a lot of time and effort if you just gave us the benefit of your knowledge with a quick lecture right now.'

'Would you like me to actually write out the assignment for you as well?' said Phil.

Maggie leaned on his arm and gazed up at him, batting her eyelashes and breathing heavily. 'Would you, darling? I'd be *ever* so grateful.'

'Yeah,' said Phil disengaging her arm. 'And I'd be ever so stupid.'

David shouldered his rucksack as they crossed the road. 'I wonder if Kirsty will remember about meeting me at the ice rink. Do you think our date is still on?' he asked of no one in particular.

Maggie spoke to Sarah. 'Will we try another shoe shop?'

'Not just to get David a date for the weekend, surely,' joked Phil.

'I'm destined never to have a pair of boots,' said Sarah sadly. 'The Fates are conspiring against me.'

'Never mind,' said David. 'We've got an Army career talk in school tomorrow. You can always join the death or glory boys and get a pair of boots for free.' He saluted smartly. 'Army issue, big feet. Keep them polished or you'll get slung in the slammer.' He stopped abruptly in the middle of the street and clicked his heels together.

An old man who had been coming along behind them walked right into him. 'Young layabout,' he said crossly. 'Too busy lying in doorways to do any work.'

'Here, Grandad!' David called after him. 'Give us ten pence for a cup of tea.'

'Behave yourself, boy,' Maggie scolded him in mock severity. 'Or, at least, if you're not going to, then don't hang about with us.' She glanced at her watch. 'It's nearly time I was off to do my three hours at the chippie. Some of us don't have easy jobs like child-minding.' She looked at Sarah. 'Do you want to try any of the big stores in the mall before I catch my bus?'

Sarah shook her head. 'I've gone off shopping just at the moment. I can't get the noise of that girl screaming out of my head.'

'Yes,' said Maggie. She shivered. 'I know what you mean. Though Phil's probably right. We'll find out later that it's been nothing serious, just something silly that set her off, and she was having some kind of hysterical fit.'

The four friends looked at each other. Without saying anything they all knew that none of them believed this.

3 Newsflash

The red light on the answering machine was flashing when Sarah got home. She clicked the tape on as she took her jacket off and hung it in the hall cupboard. Three messages, all from her mother, asking her to call her at the health centre. Sarah made herself a sandwich and dialled the number.

'Darling,' her mum said as she picked the phone up, 'I've been ringing on and off for the last hour. I wanted to catch you before you heard the news.' She paused. 'Did you hear what happened up at Crosston this afternoon?'

Sarah drew in her breath. Crosston! A sudden picture of the sales assistant, Kirsty, came into her head. Of the girl holding the telephone out, as far away from her as possible. 'No,' said Sarah. 'What happened?' But even before her mother spoke, Sarah knew it had to do with the shoe shop, the terrible screaming, and the noise of the hysterical girl on the other end of the telephone line earlier.

'There was a bomb explosion,' her mother said slowly. 'I don't like to tell you this over the phone, but I was worried you would hear of it elsewhere and think that your aunt Florrie might be involved. I've telephoned her and they were all at home when it went off. So they are quite safe, but the shops were very busy – late opening Thursday night – and there are a lot of people injured. Your dad phoned me as soon as he got his call out. He's up there just now with rest of the paramedics.'

Sarah's heart jumped. 'Dad . . . ?' The word was a question.

Her mother's voice came fast in reply, reassuring, 'He's fine, don't worry. They weren't alerted until after the bomb had exploded.'

There was a pause, and then a silence. Sarah knew what her mother was thinking. How her father would be when he eventually did come home. His work with the ambulance service meant that he often arrived late or in the early hours of the morning looking drained and exhausted.

'I'll see what's in the freezer,' said Sarah, 'and make something that can be reheated for him later if he's held up.'

There was another silence on the telephone. Then her mum's voice. 'Thanks, Sarah. You're a good girl. Oh, did you go and look for boots after school today?'

'Ah . . .' Sarah thought quickly. She didn't want to alarm her mother by telling her about the telephone call in the shoe shop. She was sure her mum would only flap and make her call the police to report it. 'Umm . . .' she said, 'there's a bit of a story about that. I'll tell you later.'

'Did Maggie go with you to help you choose?'

'Yes. *And* David, *and* Phil,' Sarah added. And then was immediately sorry that she had.

'Phil,' her mum repeated at once. 'He's that tall boy isn't he? Quite attractive, with dark eyes. I'm sure his mother comes into the health centre with his younger sister. You've been out with him before, haven't you?'

Aaaargh! Parents! Sarah mouthed the words silently at the ceiling and then took the telephone receiver and pretended to strangle it slowly.

'No, mother,' she said firmly, at last. 'I have *not* been out with him before. We went on the French exchange trip at the same time in the company of twenty others. And I was not *out* with him today either. We all went to the shops together because David and Phil had an hour to spare before rugby. And for your information Phil was much more interested in his poetry book than me.'

'Really?' said her mother. She laughed. 'How dare he? You are infinitely more interesting than any old poetry book. I'm surprised he could keep his attention on a poem with you around.'

Well, Sarah thought as she hung up the phone, that wasn't quite true. Phil had replaced his poetry book in his rucksack and then taken her arm to cross the road. And he hadn't let go of it on reaching the other side, not in fact until they had separated at the traffic lights. With David that could mean anything, everything or nothing. The eternal chat-up merchant. But with Phil . . .

She sighed as she rummaged in the deep-freeze. She didn't know what to think. Was he interested? Maggie seemed to think so. Did she even want him to be? She smiled without realising it. Yes, she supposed was the answer to that question. But she had so much work to do this year for exams and all the rest of it. Her future had to be sorted out, decisions made on which college or university would be best. The main problem was that she didn't know what she wanted to do with her life. The rest of her friends had very clear ideas. David had already made up his mind to go into leisure management, Phil would do English Lit. and Maggie, for as long as Sarah could remember, had her heart set on being a lawyer.

Her problem was, as her guidance teacher had pointed

out, that she was fairly good at many things. Sport, music, maths, English; she liked them all. She had never excelled at any one thing in particular, but with a bit of *effort* got by in them all. It made a career choice all the more difficult. She knew that she wanted to move away from home for her university life. Her mum and dad both agreed with this. It wasn't that she felt suffocated by her family, as some of her friends said they were. Despite being an only child she knew she had a lot of freedom and didn't think that she was lonely, or a solitary person. It was more a case of her being aware that there was more to see outside of the town where she lived. She knew that she would miss them both terribly though, and that itself was making her dither about her choices. The careers advisor had taken to stopping her in the corridor 'just for a little chat', but really in order to remind her that the university applications had to be sent off soon.

She decided that she would go along to the library tomorrow and do some serious investigation among the college prospectuses and university handbooks.

While the potatoes simmered on the hob, Sarah switched on the news. She was still watching the broadcast when her mother came in.

'Oh, dear,' said Mrs Bell. She stood behind Sarah as the distressing scenes from the Crosston bomb outrage were flashed across the screen. There was speculation among a studio panel as to the instigators of the crime.

'I hope this is not a bombing campaign in the lead up to Christmas,' said Mrs Bell.

'And now a report from outside the shop itself,' said the newsreader. Sarah and her mother saw the scenes of devastation in the Crosston shopping centre.

'The explosive device was placed directly below the shoe shop, the biggest retail outlet in the mall,' said the reporter. 'A deliberate act to cause the maximum possible damage by fire, and with complete disregard for human life.'

As the camera panned back and the blackened shopfront came into view, showing the extent of the damage, Sarah could see quite distinctly the piles of boots and shoes amid the broken glass.

She suddenly felt quite shaky. 'I sort of knew about that,' she said. And then she told her mother of the incident with the sales assistant in Longheath.

'What!' said her mum. Her face paled. 'Do you want to talk about it?'

Sarah twisted her hair through her fingers. 'I don't know,' she said. 'You don't ever think it will happen to you. It has made me think about the consequences of someone doing that. I suppose the Army have to deal with it eventually.' She frowned. 'They're giving a career talk in school tomorrow.'

'Your aunt Florrie or any of your cousins might have been shopping there tonight,' said her mum. She looked at Sarah's face. 'Best not to think about it just now I suppose.' She gave Sarah a quick hug and kissed her forehead. 'Let's switch this off and have dinner,' she said briskly. 'What have you made? Not refried beans again?'

It was strange, Sarah thought as she ate her dinner. In any other circumstances she wouldn't have bothered watching news details of a bomb explosion. She felt a sharp flash of guilt. Probably she would have changed channels . . . settled down to catch up with the latest episode of her favourite soap. But now that she knew where it had happened . . . was familiar with those very streets . . .

She thought of the girl on the telephone. What was her name? They had heard Kirsty saying it . . . Susan, yes Sarah was sure it had been Susan. It had personalised it for her. Now it mattered to her if Susan was all right. She hoped her dad might be able to tell her later. She glanced at her mum. 'What time do you think Dad will get in tonight?'

Her mum sighed, 'Goodness knows.'

Sarah's dad's face was shadowed and grim when he eventually did come home. He sat on the couch with a mug of tea while Sarah's mum massaged the back of his neck.

'Shall I heat up your dinner?' Sarah offered.

He shook his head. 'I'm not really hungry love. In fact,' he lifted the mug a little, 'I'm only drinking this for the sake of something to do.'

'Was it awful?' said Sarah. She sat beside him and snuggled up close.

He put one arm round her shoulder. 'Pretty bad,' he said. 'It was a miracle all the shoe shop staff got out. Glass makes a terrible mess. It gets in people's hair, cuts their faces and hands. There were a lot of very badly shocked people.' He put his mug of tea down wearily. 'I had to tend the young constable who had been on street patrol at the time. He was gibbering, like a shellshock case.'

'How can people do this?' asked Sarah's mum. 'I mean it's different if they attack an Army barracks or a defence post somewhere, but to choose a soft target like that . . . it's disgusting. There could have been any number of children about.'

'I suppose logically it is the best thing to do,' said Sarah.

'Sarah!' exclaimed her mother.

'Well, think about it. If you want to shock people and attract a lot of attention, then something like this works, in a horrible sort of a way. That's what terrorism is all about. You use violence to intimidate and frighten the population then the government is forced to listen.'

'Perhaps,' said Sarah's dad. 'But in this case, listen to whom? According to the policeman I spoke to, their intelligence section say there's no one claiming it. It wasn't associated with any known group. They have no pattern to follow, no source, no information to work on.'

Sarah's mother frowned. 'You mean it might be personal? A vendetta?'

'Something like that,' said Mr Bell. 'A lone nutcase. Who knows?' He got up slowly. 'I'm off to bed now, I'll do my reports in the morning.'

As Sarah gathered up the tea mugs and stacked them in the dishwasher her mind came back to the same question her mother had voiced earlier: what kind of person plants a bomb when they know that innocent people might be about when it goes off? Who would do a thing like like that?

High in the Lammermuir Hills Cal smoked a slow cigarette. The car window was rolled down, and an early night frost made the trembling stars wink out in the black above. On the car radio the music programme was interrupted to bring an updated news bulletin on the explosion. Cal listened, frowning. Then reached out, turned it off and flicked the cigarette end out into the night. It fell by the roadside and glowed for a moment or two before fading as the car drove away.

4 Forces network

All the talk in the school the next day was of the bombing. Sarah and her friends were less inclined to chat about it. They felt, as Maggie said, almost involved.

Even David was less flippant than usual. 'I'm going down to the shops at lunchtime to talk to Kirsty,' he said. 'See if she's OK. She must have felt pretty rough when she found out exactly what was going on during her phone call.'

In the English class Mr Eliott mentioned it as they began to discuss the literature of the First World War.

'In times of war,' he said, 'any atrocity is possible.'

'But this is not really war, sir, is it?' said Maggie. 'I mean we're not actually at war in Britain.'

'*They* think it is,' said David. 'Terrorist groups say they are fighting a war on behalf of the people. To them it's a just cause.'

'It can't be a just cause if you kill indiscriminately,' said Sarah. 'Can it?' She looked around the room at her friends, and it occurred to her that they might not have an opinion, wouldn't even have thought about it at all. And before yesterday she would have been the same; unaffected, untouched by an incident which was only a news item. But now . . . 'You would have to ask the IRA or the PLO that question,' said Mr Eliott. 'Anyway, we are discussing the War Poets, if you care to make some notes.'

'This *is* relevant, sir,' said Phil.

Mr Eliott grinned and hitched himself up on to one of the front desks. 'Oh, yeah?' he said. 'Do tell me, Philip, in what way is it relevant?'

'A lot of later criticism of Rupert Brooke's poetry focuses on his romantic illusion and the glamourisation of the sacrifices of battle. And there's no doubt that the civilians at the time were encouraged to believe in the nobility of death. Most people have absolutely no idea about the reality of war. But an incident like yesterday shows how awful violence can be.'

'Are you a pacifist, Phil?' asked Maggie.

He thought for a moment. 'Probably.'

'At any price?'

'I think so.'

'And so do I,' said Con Piers.

A row broke out among the sixth year English group.

'No way,' said Anne Tait. There were murmurs of agreement. 'Just think what would have happened in Bosnia if nobody had resisted. Genocide and widespread abuse of women and children.'

Sarah watched Phil closely. His colour was high, but there was a mulish look on his face. She had noticed this before in debate. Even if he was in the minority, he would always hold to his opinion. Steadfast, that was how her gran would describe Phil. And Sarah knew that she could relate to someone with that quality. She smiled across the room at him.

'I think that violence is unjustifiable,' said Phil.

'That's what Wilfred Owen eventually came to think,' interrupted Mr Eliott. He picked up one of his books and flipped open a page. 'At first he was keen to be off to the war, and got posted to the Front just after the Battle of the Somme. But to see the result of so much carnage had a devastating effect upon him. The sights of no-man's-land appalled him. Then he took part in the advance on the Hindenburg Line and suffered shellshock. He was sent back for rest in Craiglockhart War Hospital in Edinburgh and wrote these words to his mother: "Passivity at any price! Suffer dishonour and disgrace; but never resort to arms. Be bullied, be outraged, be killed; but do not kill."'

'Exactly,' said Phil. 'Ordinary people are encouraged by their leaders to fight, and governments exploit sentiment to do this.'

'You're an anarchist, Phil,' said Anne.

'No I'm not! That, of course, is the great cry of politicians against conscientious objectors. I don't have any sympathy with terrorist groups . . .' Phil stopped. 'Well, I suppose I do have some sympathy with some of their aims. But I utterly condemn their methods.'

'I think we'll stop getting at Philip,' said Mr Eliott. 'Did you know that Siegfried Sassoon, another War Poet whom I'd like you to study, was almost court-martialled for speaking out against militarism? But,' he added swiftly, 'we'll leave further discussion for your lesson next week.' He pointed to the pile of books on his desk. 'Take what you need from there to complete your work, or borrow from the library. The librarian assures me she has this subject very well covered.'

'Oh, by the way,' he called after them as they filed out of his classroom, 'enjoy your career talk this afternoon. I believe the British Army are having a recruiting drive.'

* * *

'ARMY CAREER ADVICE' proclaimed the poster on the door of the lecture room.

'This is *not* a recruiting drive,' began the older Army officer. 'The army is a worthwhile career for all types of people with all kinds of abilities. There are many opportunities to develop talents, take part in activities, and visit parts of the world which would not be available to you in any other line of work. We have brought along some slides which will illustrate our presentation today.' He turned to the handsome young sergeant beside him who stepped forward and spoke.

'We go out once a year to the schools and sixth form colleges to give a general talk about our Junior Cadet Corps. It might be your only chance to have someone come and talk to you about the Army and what we do. I hope that what we have to say this afternoon will interest you enough to come along to our Army introduction nights which we are holding this autumn.' His eyes under the brim of his hat crinkled in a smile and white even teeth gleamed in his tanned face.

'Gosh,' said Maggie approvingly. 'Do you think he's specially selected to strut the stuff for the female recruits?'

'Oh, yes!' agreed one of the fifth year girls. 'This is one career talk that's not going to be boring. Uniforms are a real turn-on, aren't they?' She leaned forward and whispered to the girl in front of her. 'Check out the sergeant. Isn't he drop-dead gorgeous?'

'G-L-O-W,' agreed her friend.

'Pardon?' said David. 'That's a new one on me. Anybody like to translate?'

'Good Looking – Or What?' said Maggie obligingly. She dug him in the ribs. 'You'll have to keep up with the calls, Dave, or else you'll fall behind on the Dates Rates.'

'What about tomorrow?' Sarah asked him. 'Is Kirsty coming skating?'

'I went out at lunchtime and spoke to her in the shop,' said David. 'She wants to bring Susan from the Crosston shop. She is still a bit wobbly, but Kirsty is going to try and persuade her to meet us there.' He looked at them pleadingly. 'You're all going to come along, aren't you?'

'Well we can hardly say no, now, can we?' said Sarah.

'Sshhh,' said someone as the lights were dimmed and the lecture began.

There was time for discussion and questions afterwards. Anne Tait rolled her eyes as Phil almost at once raised a point about military force.

'We also have a role as a peace-keeping force,' said the young sergeant.

'I suppose I could go along with that,' said Phil

reluctantly. 'But not everyone with a gun in their hand is a peace-keeper.'

'Absolutely not,' agreed the older man. 'There is a distinct difference in how people take up arms. We acknowledge the responsibilities and have recognised guidelines.'

'You mean an accepted code of behaviour?' asked Sarah.

'Yes. There is a Manual of Military Law under which we operate. It comes from the Declaration of St Petersburg of 1868, which itself was based on the ancient laws of chivalry. The Laws of Armed Conflict forbid non-combatant targets, such as civilians, prisoners of war, the wounded and sick. Also included are medical personnel, their vehicles and facilities and protected property, like schools or churches.'

'Well that's a relief,' said someone from the back. 'If we're ever at war again and you want to be safe, just get wounded on your way to church.'

'These "rules" don't always apply in real-life situations,' said Phil quietly.

The Army officer held his gaze. 'The British Army is one of the elite fighting forces of the world. We operate under the Hague Rules of War and the Geneva Convention. There are exceptions, of course.'

'Yes, the United Nations condemns anything that causes damage to the ecological system,' said Phil.

The officer nodded his head. 'That's true, the Protocol prohibits the use of weapons that cause widespread, long-term and severe damage to the natural environment,' he said.

'But in Vietnam and the Gulf War this was happening all the time,' Phil protested.

'And every time a space shuttle is fired it punches a huge hole in the ozone layer, and most of them have military uses,' said Maggie.

'Quite,' said the officer calmly. 'You must also appreciate there can be special battle conditions and, also, not everyone else plays by the rules. I myself was present in the Falklands when wounded British servicemen waiting to be airlifted to a hospital ship came under enemy fire. Indeed, I was one of them. I managed to get picked up by a Scout helicopter. I survived.' He paused. 'Unfortunately my best friend did not.'

There was a silence.

The sergeant smiled. 'Well, you have been a very attentive and lively group to address. If you are at all interested in making your career with the Army, and even if you're not, but you want to take a looksee, why don't you come along to the Cadet HQ for our four-week orientation course? Spend a few hours with us each Tuesday night for a month. We kick off next week at 19.00 hours.' He grinned. 'That is seven o'clock in the evening.' He picked up his papers. 'We'll hang around here for a bit in case anyone wants to ask some extra questions.'

The girl beside Maggie turned and winked at her. 'There's a few extras I'd like to interrogate him about,' she said, and she got up and walked quickly towards the rostrum.

'I'd like to give it a try,' said Sarah as they left the lecture theatre.

Phil stopped dead in front of her in the corridor. 'You're joking. Join the death or glory boys?'

Sarah flushed. 'It sounds interesting,' she said defensively.

David linked his arm in Sarah's. 'It was the boots, wasn't it?' He wagged his finger at her. 'Don't try to deny it. I was watching you when he began to talk about the free kit. He went through the list, flak jacket, beret, trousers, boots . . . As soon as the word "boots" was mentioned your face lit up. Positively glowed in fact.'

Sarah laughed. 'Can't hide much from you David, can I?'

'Nope,' agreed David. 'And I'm coming along with you next Tuesday. I always wanted to have my face blacked up just like Action Man. How about you Maggie? Would you like the British Army to make a man of you?'

'I sincerely hope not! But I have always fancied one of those wee berets. Yes, I'll go.'

The three of them looked at Phil.

'Why don't you come along, Phil?' asked Sarah.

He looked right at her, his dark eyes serious, thoughtful.

'Won't you come?' she repeated. It was a nudge rather than a push, a suggestion for him to accompany her in something she wanted to do. 'You have to concede that the Army does help out when there is a state of emergency or a disaster.'

He smiled at her then and said, 'OK, Sarah Bell, I'll come along. And you'd better watch out. You might find that I can outrun and outgun all of you.'

5 Special supplies

Sarah went to meet her mother at the health centre after school. Her mum finished early on Friday nights and they would usually go around the shops together for an hour or so before going home. But when Sarah arrived at the health centre her mum was still working in her office at the back.

'What's all this?' asked Sarah, waving her hand at the boxes stacked in the corner.

'Special supplies, just arrived,' her mother said briefly. She frowned as she rifled through a bundle of invoices. 'Look give me a minute or two, Sarah. I'll need to check these off before I go.'

'Why not leave them until Monday?'

'I can't. They have to be marked off and stored at once.'

'Here, I'll give you a hand.' Sarah took a few from the top of the pile and picked up a pen from her mother's desk.

'No, don't,' said her mother quickly. She pulled the invoices from Sarah's hand. 'You go and read a magazine in the waiting area or . . . or better still, go and buy something from the shops.' She took her purse out and shoved a twenty-pound note into Sarah's hand.

'What?' Sarah looked at the money in her hand. 'What's the matter with you tonight? You normally can't wait to leave here on a Friday. It's usually coat on and keys in hand by the time I get here.' She looked at her mother more closely. 'Is there anything wrong?'

'No. Not at all. There's a bit of extra work, that's all. And I'm a little harassed, so I'd probably get through it faster on my own.'

'No you wouldn't,' said Sarah reasonably. 'You do one lot and I'll do the other and we'll be finished in half the time.' She reached out for the invoices.

Her mother snatched them away. 'I think it's too complicated for you to manage, Sarah,' she said sharply.

'Really!' Sarah started to laugh. 'I've helped you out with stuff like this before. What's so complicated this time?' She stared at her mother hard. 'Are you going to tell me, or do I have to drag it out of you?' She grinned at her mother. 'I'm bigger than you now, remember?'

'Oh! You always were a nosy child,' her mother said in exasperation.

'Inquisitive,' corrected Sarah. 'Child psychologists refer to it as being inquisitive. It's a sign of intelligence.'

Her mother flopped down in a chair. 'This is strictly confidential,' she said. Sarah nodded. 'All the health centres around here have had special consignments delivered. The doctors and the paramedics have to carry extras for the time being.'

'Why?' asked Sarah. She went over to the boxes in the corner.

Her mother heaved a sigh. 'Oh, it happens from time to time. If there's an outbreak of a disease say, like a measles epidemic.'

'Yeah, but this is different, isn't it?' said Sarah. She knelt down and examined one of the cartons. 'This is not for a flu outbreak, or you wouldn't be so jittery.'

'Well, the administrators here think it's strange,' said her mum. She ran her fingers through her hair. 'By grapevine gossip and the type of materials which are arriving, we believe the authorities are anticipating something else.'

'For instance?'

'Something like Crosston. Maybe worse.'

They looked at each other.

'So what exactly are in these boxes?' asked Sarah.

'Body bags,' said her mother.

Gran came for dinner that night. Friday night was always special in Sarah's house. Dad brought in carry-out Chinese or Indian and they spread themselves in front of the open fire in the living-room and settled down. Gran was coming to stay, so that made it even better, thought Sarah. She didn't mind sharing her room every other weekend. Ever since she had been little her gran always brought her some small gift, and hadn't stopped even when Sarah had become older. Sometimes it was something completely wild like a horrendous lipstick, but then the next month it would be something unusual – a seashell or an old book. She knew that now she should be much too mature for that sort of thing, but she couldn't help the small, secret, pleased feeling that she had when they heard the taxi arriving outside the house.

She always ran and hugged her gran. 'And how's my Copper Kitten this week?' her gran asked, using her own pet name for Sarah. She reached up and stroked the long copper-coloured curls of Sarah's hair.

'So, so,' said Sarah.

'Did we get our boots at last?' said the old lady. She winked at Sarah. She had added ten pounds to Sarah's boot fund on her last visit.

'It's in hand.' Sarah took her gran's bag and slung it in her room. 'I've got something to discuss with you. I need some objective advice.' They settled themselves in the living-room while Sarah's mum and dad set out the food. 'I'm considering a career with the Army,' said Sarah. She was watching her parents closely.

Her mother looked up in surprise. 'You never told us.'

'It only happened today. It was one of our careers talks. They do an orientation course one night a week over four weeks. You can go along and see if you like it and then they have a selection weekend.'

'A selection weekend? What's that?' asked Sarah's dad.

'It's where Sarah gets to select the most handsome young man,' said Gran at once.

Her dad laughed. 'That sounds OK to me. Does a reciprocal arrangement work for the boys?'

'Oh, be serious,' said Sarah's mother. 'Are you quite keen on this, Sarah?' She frowned. 'I hope they haven't turned your head with all the razzmatazz of the uniform and the *esprit de corps* propaganda.'

'Sarah's far too sensible to be lured away by any of the superficial aspects,' said her dad.

'They did make it sound a lot of fun,' said Sarah. 'But no, I think I'm attracted for other reasons, too. I like the idea of a unit dedicated to the service of your country.'

Her parents exchanged glances.

'People get killed serving their country,' said her mother.

Sarah's dad laid his hand on her mum's arm. 'We don't want to put you off, Sarah. I'm sure it is a worthwhile job, but it could be dangerous.'

'Well, I'd like to try it out. But . . . you see we are studying the War Poets in English at the moment and it raised a lot of discussion on the ethics of warfare and . . . Phil said . . .'

'Ah,' said Sarah's mother. 'Phil . . .'

'Oh, for goodness sake. It wasn't him in particular. A lot of people were talking about the fact that it was all a con.'

'About the glory of war?' said Gran. 'About the honour of dying for one's country. "If I should die, think only this of me . . ." That's a poem by Rupert Brooke, you know.'

'Yes,' said Sarah slowly. She suddenly remembered Gran's two older brothers had been killed in the First World War. 'Sorry Gran. I forgot that . . .' Sarah looked at her mum and dad for help.

'It's all right, dear,' Gran took Sarah's hand in her own. 'It was a long time ago, a *very* long time ago, and I was only a little girl. Yet . . . sometimes I recall them as though it were only yesterday. Harry was good natured, always joking, always had time for me, would play the silliest games, humour me with my dolly tea parties. And Bob, he was the dour one, never spoke a word unless forced, and then only three at a time. But . . . he always had a sweet in his pocket for me. He would never say anything, mind, just catch my eye and point to his jacket hanging on the back of the door. And then he would give me a nod and I would slide down from the table when my parents weren't looking . . .' Sarah's gran smiled. 'When they came marching through our village with the pipes and drums there wasn't one young man who didn't enlist, narry a one. They were desperate to get away. The Lord God himself could not have contained them. And we were proud that saw them go. It was the right thing to do. To serve your country. But . . . they never came back again. Not a single one.'

There was a long silence in the room.

Sarah's gran looked around the room. But it was as if she was seeing a landscape that didn't exist any more. 'Who knows?' she sighed. And then she turned to Sarah and smiled. 'It's all different now, pet, anyway. They need peace-keepers, and, as you say, it's a career. If I were you I'd go along and see what's what.'

Later Sarah overheard her mum and dad talking in the kitchen as they cleared up after supper.

'Is your paramedic unit receiving special supplies?' her mum asked her dad.

Mr Bell looked at his wife. 'You too?' he queried.

Sarah's mum nodded. 'Disaster stuff,' she said. 'Morphine, body bags, the lot. The talk is that there's a terrorist unit operating somewhere close by.'

Sarah's dad put his arm round her shoulder. 'I wouldn't get too worried if I were you,' he said. 'I've been in this business a bit longer than you. It's probably just a precaution.'

'Perhaps not. Perhaps the police have been able to trace something from Crosston.'

Sarah's dad laughed. 'Knowing our boys in blue, if they are hot on the trail, this should mean that the terrorists are probably sunning themselves in South America by now.'

'They must know something,' insisted Sarah's mother.

Her dad shrugged. 'Maybe. It could be an anonymous tip-off.'

'Yes, and you know who has to follow up these tip-offs?' said his wife tightly. 'You know who is given the task of clearing the streets while a bomb might be ticking away . . . ?'

'You're thinking of the Army, aren't you?' said Sarah's dad. 'And of our only child, our little girl's life under threat.'

'Wouldn't you worry if she joined up?'

'Yes. But we've talked about this before, haven't we? We

agreed that we wouldn't prevent her from finding her own way in life.' He smiled at his wife. 'Come on, help me with the coffee.'

They came back through to the living-room and the talk turned to the bombing outrage at Crosston.

'Thank God that Florrie and the children weren't shopping that night,' said Gran.

'Yes,' said Sarah's mum. 'It's just luck really that there were no casualties.'

Her dad picked up the evening newspaper. 'I suppose you could count one. A middle-aged man had a heart attack just outside the shopping centre. He had left his daughter shopping there, so they believe it might not be entirely unconnected.' He put the newspaper aside. 'On our call-out report it will still be listed as "No casualties".'

'No casualties.' Cal stared at the headline and spat out the words. There was a mocking tone to the article, a decided smugness, as though the enemy had been outwitted. Well, the next time would have to be arranged so that they would not escape scot-free.

Those tabloids trying to appear more knowledgeable mentioned a team of bombers. Cal screwed up the paper viciously. A *team* of bombers. Others taking the credit. They would have to be shown. The next target would have to be more outrageous. And also . . . people should know that this wasn't any ordinary bomber. The name of the bombed town stood out in bold letters on the page . . . Crosston. Perhaps there was a way to make the next one more meaningful also . . .

6 Incident aftermath

By the time Sarah met her friends at the ice rink in the local Pyramid Centre the group numbered about a dozen. David had persuaded some other classmates and assorted friends to come along. It was fun to be out on the ice in the evening, thought Sarah. The music blared out a thumping beat through the loudspeakers, and the whole gang was having a great time, laughing and clowning about.

After half an hour had passed the tempo switched to traditional dance and old-fashioned waltz music. David suggested a Come Dancing competition, and they all started to pair off haphazardly.

Suddenly Phil skated up fast beside Sarah and took her arm. 'I think we could win this,' he said. He grasped her firmly round her waist and brought her close beside him as they sped past David, who had appointed himself judge.

'They don't hold their partners as closely as that on the telly,' shouted David.

Phil grinned at David. 'Jealous!' he shouted back.

'Watch it,' David called after them. 'You two will get disqualified for enjoying yourselves.'

Sarah had to skate hard to keep up with Phil. Being almost the same height they were quite well matched, but he was fitter and faster than she. The speed at which they were travelling made the wind whip at her face and her hair stream out behind. As they came round the second time, Phil slowed down, and then, catching her with both hands round her waist, he lifted her into the air and swung her in a circle.

'Bravo!' cried Maggie as she zoomed past them holding on to Con's hand. Without thinking Sarah let go Phil's arm to wave at her friend. The next second she was on her bottom on the ice. Phil landed just beside her.

'Neel pwans,' yelled David in an atrocious French accent.

'Yechhh!' said Sarah. She got up slowly and surveyed her jeans. 'I'm soaked. I want to go and sit out for a bit.'

'I was fouled,' complained Phil as he limped off beside her.

Sarah sat down on the benches at the side. Truthfully she was rather glad to take a rest. Her breath was coming in gasps and frosting in the air. Phil sat down beside her.

'You were showing off,' she accused him.

'True. But look at them.' Phil waved his hand at the rest of the skaters. 'Dull and boring and ordinary, merely going round and round. Better to do something spectacular and die in the attempt.'

'Oh, very good,' said Sarah. 'But perhaps in future you could consult your partner first.'

Phil turned quickly to face her. 'Is that how you see yourself then? As my partner?'

Sarah gasped. 'I didn't mean that. Sorry, I . . .' She broke off, unsure what to say next.

'Oh, don't be.' Phil gave her a long look. 'I'm not.'

Sarah turned her head away. Now she was completely confused. What was he doing to her? Flirting as much as David one minute, and then deadly serious the next.

They watched the skating for a few minutes, then Phil stood up. 'Want to have another go?'

'You carry on. I'll sit out for a bit longer.' She waved him away and watched him step back on to the ice and effortlessly glide off. She really was quite unfit, she decided. Certainly compared to him. She would have to go for a run and perhaps do some swimming before next Tuesday, or else she would show up badly in any kind of exercise she might be involved in.

She watched her friends as they skated. David, the natural comic, was fooling around, yet was also managing to chat up Kirsty and A. N. Other simultaneously. Maggie and Con seemed to be getting on very well, although Maggie got on well with everybody. She was the most good natured of them all, coaxing Phil out of his moods and tolerating David's endless chatter when no one else could be bothered with him.

Sarah loved coming here at the weekends. Bright and airy, it was known as the Pyramid Centre because of the huge triangular glass canopy which encompassed the ice rink and the rest of the shopping centre. It was a landmark in the town, a favourite meeting place. Sarah looked up at the apex of the triangle reaching high above her. On a Saturday afternoon the whole place was thronged with people. Old, young, children in buggies, kids spending pocket money, folks meeting to eat in one of the food outlets which surrounded the actual ice rink. In a few more weeks Christmas shopping would begin in earnest and the mall would be absolutely full.

For no reason at all a thought came into Sarah's head – this would be a bomber's paradise. With all the boots, coats, jackets and holdalls lying here and there, it was the perfect place to leave a parcel. In the mêlée of kids changing, parents watching, teenagers dating, people snacking, waiting their turn, or resting, it would go unnoticed. And the effect it would have . . . Sarah's eyes swept round in a circle. Somewhere like this would be an ideal target for the type of person who had planted the bomb at Crosston. Sarah looked up again at the huge roof, composed of hundreds of interconnecting pieces of shaped glass. She imagined the glass splintering into thousands of pieces, falling . . .

'Absolutely catastrophic,' she said aloud.

There was a flash of blades, and Phil's face, ruddy with a healthy glow, appeared at the barrier.

'Dave's suggesting going for a pizza and then the cinema afterwards. Are you on?'

'Sure. Except he doesn't get to pick what we see. The last film outing he organised was vile. Reservoir Rats meets Showgirl Cats, or some other item geared towards brain-dead blokes.'

'Well Maggie's not choosing either,' said Phil. 'She invariably wants some nauseating yuck with a Disney dimension.'

'Nothing wrong with a good Disney film,' said Sarah. 'I myself have a Lion King pencil-case, and don't mind admitting it.'

Phil glanced quickly around. 'If you promise not to tell anyone I'll let you in on a little secret.' He leaned over the barrier and lowered his voice. 'I have on occasion borrowed my wee sister's Pocahontas bubble bath.'

Sarah laughed out loud. 'We may have a problem getting the others to agree with our choice.'

'I'll go and buy an evening paper, and hopefully we can reach a compromise.'

Sarah watched him skate off. He was very good looking and athletic, but with a thoughtful, gentle side to him that she was becoming more and more attracted to.

She made her way round to where the rest of her friends sat unlacing their skates. Susan, from the shoe shop in Crosston, had arrived earlier. Her face was cut and grazed and her arm was bandaged. She hadn't joined in the skating but seemed content to stand and watch. As Sarah came up she was talking about the bombing.

'I don't remember much about it. The floor exploded only metres away from where I was standing talking to Kirsty on the telephone. The firemen said the fact that the basement was so deep and the roof so strong saved us.' She wiped her hand over her eyes. 'All I could hear was someone screaming . . . and then I realised it was me.'

'Head Office have been really helpful,' said Kirsty. 'They've all got paid leave until the shop opens again.'

'I'm so nervous now,' said Susan. 'Not sleeping at night. I keep thinking that everybody I meet might be a killer. I find myself staring at people in crowds thinking they might be the one.'

'Didn't anyone notice anything suspicious that afternoon?' Maggie asked her.

Susan shook her head. 'The police keep asking that. Whoever it was must have walked right past us at the desk. One of the other sales assistants remembers this young guy hanging about. She gave them a description, but it was very vague.'

'You'll just have to try and forget it,' Maggie told her. 'Put it out of your mind.'

'What I can't believe is that he never gave any warning,' said Susan. '*And* the fire alarm had been tampered with, so that it didn't ring in the fire station. It was pure luck that no one was right down in the basement when it went off. If our security guard hadn't been really fast on his feet . . .' She shuddered. 'He practically threw us all out of the shop.'

Sarah looked at the girl's white face. She found it difficult to know what to say. She was seeing first hand one of the effects of terrorism. A young girl, who previously had enjoyed her perfectly normal existence, nights out with her friends, now traumatised and distressed. There have to be security forces, thought Sarah, to try to prevent or contain violent actions, and some sections of them, such as the Army, need to be armed.

She looked up gratefully as Phil came back with a copy of the evening paper. He glanced quickly at her and, sensing her mood, gave the newspaper to David. He sat down beside them and began to chat easily. Sarah felt some of the tension ebb away and, as her eyes met Phil's, she realised that he was being kind. She suddenly thought that she might love someone for that quality alone.

'Right,' said David, turning the pages of the newspaper. 'Let's see what the grand metropolis of Longheath is offering filmgoers this weekend.'

'Oh look,' said Maggie, as he flicked through the pages. 'There's an ad for the Marines. Give us that David while you look up the film listings.'

David shook out the page and handed it to her.

'It says here you can prove yourself with the Marines,' said Maggie. She began to read out the advert in a deep commanding voice. '"We need people, but they must be the right people ..."'

'That's us,' said David. 'We are *definitely* the right people.'

'"The training is intense ..."'

'I'll be very intense,' said Con. He set his face in a serious frown, shaded his eyes with his hand, and gazed resolutely out across the ice.

'"... and professional,"' said Maggie.

Con leaped to his feet and clicked his heels. 'This do?' he asked.

Maggie studied them critically. She shook her head sadly. 'I think you'll need some extra training. But wait!' She held up her hand. 'It says here that there will be further training given, and it will put you in the best mental and physical shape of your life. You will learn advanced survival techniques . . .'

'Nobody needs to give me advice on my technique,' David interrupted her. He grinned and slipped one arm round Kirsty's shoulder. Maggie made a face, rolling her eyes about, and Kirsty laughed.

Sarah took the article and began to read down the page. 'After the explosion up at Crosston,' she said, 'I'm beginning to take this a bit more seriously.'

7 Soldier, Soldier

'There's the boots, Sarah,' said David immediately as they entered the Army drill hall on Tuesday night. He dug Sarah in her ribs. 'What d'ye reckon?'

Sarah smiled and poked him back. 'I reckon that after a few days square-bashing wearing them, you'd lose that perfectly groomed hairstyle David.'

They walked towards the exhibition at the end of the hall. Photographs and pictures showed the Army in action and featured all aspects of Army life, from cook to bandsman. In the centre was a full-size model of a soldier in combat dress. They went round slowly, looking at the display boards and examining the radio, the weapons, and other uniforms which were on show.

Sarah came back to the figure of the kneeling

commando. 'The coveted red beret,' she said.

Phil came up behind her. 'Will I check the boot size?' he whispered in her ear. 'And if they're OK, we'll just nick them and go.'

'Enough,' laughed Sarah. She pushed him towards the row of chairs which were set out at the front. 'Sit down and listen to the presentation quietly.'

'Well, that takes care of the skiing in Norway, the lazing around the beaches in Cyprus and the comradeship in being one of the boys,' said Phil fifteen minutes later. He sat back and folded his arms. 'This is all sales talk.'

'Yeah,' said Maggie, 'and it's working. Look.' She nudged Phil's arm and nodded towards Sarah at the end of the row. Sarah was leaning forwards paying close attention to every word. Phil sighed and ran his fingers through his hair.

The young sergeant wound up his speech. 'Stick with us for the next four weeks. Each Tuesday will be a new experience for you and each one different from the previous one. Those evenings, combined with one extra day out on field exercises, that's all of your time that we ask. Then at the end of it, if you're still keen, come along on the selection weekend.'

'What's the selection weekend?' asked David.

'You are taken away for a weekend later on in

December to our base at Catterick. We camp out, do some basic training, command tasks, night manoeuvres. You attend lectures and seminars which will give you a fuller insight into Army life. We hold active discussion-group meetings, which will help clarify your own thoughts. It's pretty tough, but it lets us see who shapes up and who doesn't. Then we have a good night in the mess before we set off for home in the morning.'

'He makes it all sound rather jolly,' said Maggie.

'I think it sounds masochistic,' said David.

'Right,' said the sergeant. 'We're going to divide you up into more manageable numbers. This will be your training team, and one of the third year cadets will be assigned to look after each set of people. Just form a group with your friends if that's easiest, say about four or five in each.'

Sarah, David, Maggie and Phil separated off, and a third year cadet called Ben was sent across to sort them out. 'We'll grab the far end of the hall,' he said, 'and set up some activities.' He called over a couple of second year cadets and then sent Maggie, David and Sarah off with them to help bring the equipment from store, while he and Phil cleared one end of the hall.

'Looking forward to the weekend at Catterick?' he asked Phil.

'I don't know if I'll even stay these first four weeks,' said Phil. 'It's all a bit too yah for me.'

'You mean you can't hack it?' said Ben.

'Perhaps I just don't want to,' said Phil.

'Why are you here then?' asked Ben.

'Why are you?' countered Phil.

Ben laughed. 'Truthfully? I came a couple of years ago because the girl I fancied was coming.'

Then Phil laughed too. 'I am quite interested in what the role of the Army might be in the modern world, but you could say that somebody influenced my decision to come along.'

'Ah,' said Ben. He looked around the hall and his eyes found Sarah. 'Let me guess,' he said. 'The one with the long copper-coloured hair?'

Phil shrugged. 'We're just pals. She's OK.'

'Mmmm,' said Ben. He put his head on one side. 'I'd say she was a bit more than OK. Come on, mate, let's get you started on the assault course, and you can show her how smart you are.'

While Ben asked them to gather round and began to explain what they had to do, some of the second year cadets set up various pieces of apparatus. 'It's a straightforward old-fashioned obstacle race,' said Ben. 'It will do as a very basic fitness test. You're going to have to run, jump, roll over, swing on the rope, make up a piece of simple kit, dismantle it again and then race for the finishing line . . . which we'll put . . . there.' He indicated a line drawn out at the far end of the room. 'You have to complete each section before returning to base. It's a race, but nobody wins. You're not in competition with each other. You are competing against the hardest opponent you'll ever meet. Yourself.'

He looked around and beckoned to a second year cadet. 'John is going to do a tour first and give you a demo.'

The four friends watched as John easily made his way round the course and then ran back to base at the front of the hall.

'Right,' said Ben. He turned back to them. 'Now, who's first?'

Maggie was at the front. 'Eh, hold on a minute,' she said. She sauntered up to the first obstacle, a wall made of polystyrene bricks, and stood against it. She gazed upwards. 'Er . . . this,' she said pointing at the top, 'is rather larger than I am.'

'So it is,' Ben agreed cheerfully.

Maggie returned to her place at the head of the line. She gave Ben her most winning smile. 'Aren't you going to go easy on us females because we're frail and vulnerable?'

'No way,' said Ben. 'Girls are a lot tougher than most people think. *And* a lot more ruthless. During the Second

World War the French Resistance had a high proportion of young females working in active service. Women terrorists are the most feared. They are the least likely to surrender, and the most likely to knock off hostages. The unwritten rule of the anti-terrorist units during a rescue mission is shoot the women first.'

Maggie tried again. 'But I'm just a beginner,' she whined, 'and I need some help to get over that wall.'

'Over it or through it,' said Ben. 'Your choice.'

'But you do make some allowances for women, surely,' said Sarah.

'Your one concession is that you get to drink your beer out of half-pint glasses, while the men use full-pint mugs. That's it.'

'That's not a concession!' declared Sarah. 'That's discrimination!'

'I'll drink my beer from a pint glass if I want to,' said Maggie.

'Not in this mess, you won't,' said Ben.

'You don't drink beer, Maggie,' said David.

'I'll drink my Irn-Bru in pints then,' said Maggie.

'That's not the point, of course,' said Phil. 'The fact that you differentiate is sexist.'

'You could say that having a skirt as part of a dress uniform is sexist,' said Ben.

'Well so it is,' said Sarah.

Ben laughed. 'Well, on our parades the guys wear kilts, so I guess that evens it out.' He grabbed Maggie's arm. 'Now no more procrastinating. You're first. Off you go.' And he shoved her in the direction of the wall.

Sarah laughed so much her sides ached. Maggie did make a brave attempt. Even Ben had to concede that point. But after a couple of false starts she realised that she was getting nowhere, so she eventually flung herself desperately at the wall, which collapsed with a spectacular flourish. Bricks went flying everywhere, and when the last one settled, Maggie lay among them, arms and legs flung out like a starfish.

Ben put his arm out to stop anyone going to her aid, 'Come on Mags!' he shouted. 'Get up, girl!'

Slowly, with extreme dignity, Maggie rose to her feet. She dusted herself off carefully and then, with a haughty toss of her head, she marched determinedly on to the next object.

Ben followed her all the way round the course shouting encouragement. 'Good effort! Good effort!' he cried as she completed a rather ragged backwards somersault. 'Come on lass,' he spoke quietly as her fingers fumbled when setting up the camp stove. 'Go! Go! Go!' he yelled, as she hesitated with the rope in her hand on top of the box.

She grimaced and launched herself into the air to swing across the gap, misjudged the distance and dropped into netting below. It took her several minutes to distentangle herself.

As she staggered towards the last test Ben nodded to someone at the front of the room. Maggie did twenty skips, and then flung the skipping rope aside, and as she began to run down the hall to the finish, Ben raised his hand. Suddenly the Vangelis tune from *Chariots of Fire* blared out over the loudspeakers. Phil and David were doubled over with laughter, and tears were running down Sarah's face when Maggie finally crossed the line.

'I think I deserve a medal for that,' said Maggie, as she limped over to her friends and sat down.

'Well a drink at any rate,' said Ben. 'And I'll buy it for you.' He put his arm round her shoulder. 'You're a stayer, kiddo. Not many would have done that on their first training night.'

'I could have hurt myself,' Maggie complained to Ben in the mess afterwards.

'Pain is a privilege. It is weakness leaving the body,' said Ben unsympathetically. He looked at them seriously. 'You do realise that despite the fact that all of your performances were technically more slick than Maggie's, she did best tonight. It's what I meant when I said you're competing against yourself. It doesn't matter if you fall, as long as you get up again.'

Later, as Sarah prepared for bed, Ben's final words were still in her mind. It could be a philosophy for life she supposed. What was it that he had said? It's the getting up again that counts.

The concept of competing against yourself had struck a chord with Phil, too. She had discussed that with him as they walked ahead of the others to the bus stop.

'I can see the value in that kind of training,' Phil had said. 'You measure your own performance, not by any given absolute, but as a constant striving to better yourself.'

'And I suppose that's where the pride in achievement comes in,' Sarah had added. 'I mean Maggie *did* do really well. She was the first to go, which made it more difficult, and she's quite tiny compared to us, and definitely not as strong. So it was a personal triumph for her to complete the course.'

Phil had linked his arm with hers then and pulled her closer.

'Sarah, you might convince me after all that there is some merit in today's modern Army.'

8 Remember, Remember

'I've a special task for you over the weekend,' Mr Eliott told them on Friday. 'The Head has asked me to look out some suitable readings for the school's Remembrance Day service next week. And following a time-honoured custom in teaching, which is, don't do anything yourself, when you can have someone else do it for you, I decided that you lot could indulge in a bit of research and come up with your own selections.'

The class groaned.

Mr Eliott shook his head. 'I had hoped that you would all leap upon this piece of work, that you would be keen to have some input. It is an ideal opportunity for you at this moment, as it does have bearing on our study topic. In fact, I consider myself rather generous in allowing you to undertake this assignment.'

'Do we really have to?' asked David.

'Indeed you do,' said Mr Eliot. 'I told the Head that you would all be absolutely delighted to do it. And she expressed *her* delight that you were delighted, and told me how tremendously pleased she was. Now, we all know the first rule of survival in educational establishments, don't we?'

Nobody answered.

'All right, I'll tell you,' said Mr Eliott. 'Rule number one is to please the Head. Pleasing the Head wins Brownie points.' He beamed at them all. 'Oh, and it will also count towards the final mark in your assessments. So, any ideas?'

'I suppose we must have Rupert Brooke,' said Phil. He began to recite a line of poetry:

> *Now, God be thanked Who has matched us with His hour.*
> *And caught our youth, and wakened us from sleeping . . .*

'Is that what you would choose?' asked Con.

'No it isn't,' said Phil. 'That's what I'd *not* choose.'

'I rather like it,' said Maggie. 'It has a nice sort of flow. You could imagine someone on the prow of a ship or somewhere, inspiring their men with those words.'

'Yeah, a lot of his stuff has that kind of superficial appeal,' said Phil.

'I thought he was a good poet,' Con protested. 'My book says he was quoted at the time as being the poet who did justice to the nobility of our youth in arms.'

'Well, if you find romance and sentiment about war appealing, then I suppose you'd like him,' said Phil.

'Don't dismiss Brooke so swiftly, Phil,' said Mr Eliott. 'He was a talented young man with a high intellect. His travel writing, criticisms and letters are very well regarded. He probably would have developed a great deal had he lived – he was beginning to display signs of major talent. And you should bear in mind that his lines were taken up by people not only to glorify deeds in battle, but also as a consolation to help make sense of what had happened in their lives. Many of the mothers and fathers waiting at home only received the official War Office telegram. That was all. They sent away a beloved son to fight for their country, and were not even given his body back to bury.'

'Yes,' said Sarah, 'my gran says that was a most terrible heartache to her own mother. She had no grave nearby to visit and tend for her sons. It was like another bereavement. Years later, when she was still a young woman, my gran went across to France. It was a great adventure for her. And she eventually found her brothers at Bayeux. They were lying almost side by side. She said it was beautiful, very quiet and still. And the graves are so well kept there, with roses and other flowers between the crosses. She took a photograph and brought it home. It helped her mother a lot to see their resting place before she died.'

'Oh, Sarah,' said Maggie. She touched her friend's arm. 'That's a sad story.'

'There are many sad stories,' said Mr Eliott. 'Rudyard Kipling's only son was killed in action. Kipling served on the War Graves Commission to help ease his grief.'

'And I suppose that's what we do on Remembrance Sunday,' said Sarah slowly. 'Ease the grief of those left behind. I never thought of it like that before.'

'Neither did I,' said Phil. 'I always saw it as an excuse for the military to show off. Stir up national pride.'

'That does happen,' said Mr Eliott. 'We can all be seduced by the image of the brave hero. The names of Eliotts are on many of the war memorials in this area. My grandfather, his five brothers, most of their cousins, were lost in the First World War. Three of my uncles were killed in the Second World War. In a few days' time I will stand there at the service on Remembrance Sunday and I'll be very sad. But . . . I will also be very proud. And,' he sighed, 'I'm not sure why.'

'I'd like to choose a poem for peace,' said Phil.

'It doesn't necessarily have to be a poem,' said Mr Eliott. 'It can be a piece of prose, an extract from a letter, something personal, if you wish. I'll eventually take six to submit to the Head as she wants a reading by a representative from each year group. Now,' he picked up his pen. 'Has anyone got any work for me?'

Remembrance Day . . . A day to remember . . . Remember, remember, the fifth of November, gunpowder, treason and plot . . .

Cal smiled. Yes that would do. Gunpowder . . . Treason . . . Plot.

What was needed was a plot.

The papers were very helpful. A special service at Altminster. Laying of the wreath at the tomb of the Unknown Soldier by a pupil from the nearby school. All the local organisations taking part. A big turn-out expected; the uniformed groups – Cubs, Scouts, Girl Guides, Brownies, Cadets. There would be a band, and a march past. Bands were good; exciting, loud. They distracted attention, covered up noise.

And Altminster . . . Cal stared at the name. See? It was meant to be. It would fit in perfectly. Then they would understand. It was not a *team* of bombers. Just one. One to take the credit. One . . .

Cal frowned. But then this wasn't one. It was two. Hit number two. And they would have to be told that as well. Make it really clear. Two . . .

Two.

That would be more difficult. More cunning needed. Cal looked down. Hands shaking. Stop. Breathe. Excitement. Only excitement. Cal smiled again. But that was also good. Gave it an edge.

So . . .

It was settled. And they would know, wouldn't they? They wouldn't still be so stupid as to think there was a gang doing this.

But . . . just in case, it could be mentioned in the warning. Now look. Hands shaking again. The warning. Last time was bad. Left it too late. Might have been found out. So . . . do it earlier this time, and let them know . . . let them know . . . so that they would remember.

Remember . . . Remember . . .

But not the fifth. No.

Remembrance Sunday. That was much better.

Remembrance Day.

It *would* be memorable this year. Very memorable indeed.

9 Look good – Feel good

The Army were also getting ready for Remembrance Sunday. At the drill hall the following Tuesday the place was buzzing with preparations. The second year cadets who were going to take part in the ceremony for the first time were busy polishing brasses and dubbing boots.

'That looks like hard work,' said Sarah as she watched one boy rubbing and rubbing the toes of his boots in a circular motion.

'It is,' said Ben. 'It's not called bulling for nothing. But it's worth it when you see the end result.'

'Convince me,' said Maggie.

'Look good – feel good. Feel good – perform,' said Ben.

'Is that another one of the Army's catch phrases?' enquired Phil politely.

'Yes,' said Ben, 'and it's true. How you look is how you feel. And how you feel can determine how you act. So a well-turned-out soldier will perform better. It helps with morale.'

'And are parades good for morale?' asked David.

'Being in a big parade is one of the most thrilling experiences ever.' Ben's eyes were glowing. 'Ask any of the cadets who have passed out. It is something special. Once you know the drill routines and you feel confident about obeying the commands, it is a fabulous feeling to follow behind the pipes and drums and go marching through the streets.'

'I can imagine,' said Phil sarcastically.

'No you can't,' said Ben seriously. 'Really, honestly Phil, you can't, it's unbelievable. Better than when they play the anthem at the start of an international rugby match, better than any football chant. It's moving and emotional and it charges you up . . . I love it.'

'I think it could be dangerous,' said Phil. 'I don't know if I agree with charging people up like that.'

'Phil Jarvis!' cried Sarah. 'How can you say that?'

Phil turned to her. 'Because it's what I believe.'

'Is this the same boy who becomes incensed when watching rugby videos of the Grand Slam?' Sarah demanded, pointing her finger at him. 'I don't notice you switching them off and refusing to watch them again.'

'That's different,' said Phil.

'Not much,' said Sarah. 'May I also remind you of an incident on the bus returning us to the school after our outing to Edinburgh to see *Les Miserables*?'

'Ahhh . . .' said Phil.

'Exactly,' said Sarah triumphantly. 'Were you or were you not the person who purloined my red scarf, and stood up on your seat on the journey home waving it enthusiastically and singing, "Do you hear the people sing?"'

Phil laughed and stuck his tongue out at her. 'You're too clever for me, Sarah Bell,' he said. 'I give in. I suppose it must be quite thrilling to take part in something like that.'

'And to watch,' said Ben. 'Why don't you come along on Sunday? Meanwhile, tonight we're going to get you into some kit and do a couple of basic drill orders.'

'Now, Maggie is rather smartly dressed in what are known as the number twos, whereas Phil has opted for the full regalia with kilt, sporran and white spats.'

Ben was walking among them with a trailing microphone giving a running commentary as the new cadets appeared from the storeroom wearing some version of Army dress.

'Maggie has a tartan skirt, white blouse and a jacket of pale green,' he went on.

'Puke green I'd call it,' said Maggie under her breath. 'You don't seriously expect us to appear in public wearing this?' she asked Ben.

'Yes,' said Ben. 'And be proud to do it.'

Maggie held up one leg. 'How can anybody be proud of tights which are a bronzed-bimbo shade?' she asked. 'People will shout "sunbed tan" after me in the street with these on.'

Ben ignored her. 'Here comes David and he has on working dress which is used around camp and for cadet nights. Plain green shirt and trousers, plain green ribbed jumper, and beret.'

A few more people came out into the hall wearing the same outfit. 'And now for combat kit,' said Ben. 'Camouflage trousers, combat jacket, beret . . .'

Sarah was in the last group to appear. She suited the outfit and she knew it. The jacket and trousers fitted her well, and the beret sat to one side of her head, cap badge gleaming. Positioning the beret was important, the quartermaster had informed her. Held firmly in place with the three fingers of one hand, then pulled hard across with the other hand and flattened down against the side of the head.

'Sarah certainly looks the part,' said Ben.

What part? thought Phil. She might kill someone in that gear. He felt quite gloomy as he studied her.

Then Sarah saw Phil in the full military dress uniform and went over to him. 'You look rather dashing,' she said.

'Right,' said Ben when everyone had assembled in the hall. 'We'll do a quick rank and file line up, a "stand at ease" and "come to attention" and then "dismiss".'

Sarah found she enjoyed it all. First the cadets sorted themselves into three rows, and then shuffled about taking a distance of an arm's length from the person on either side and in front or behind.

'Reminds me of lining up at primary school,' muttered David.

Ben explained how to stand at ease: feet apart, hands loosely held together behind back, palms out and flat, right thumb over left thumb. 'Head up!' he shouted. 'Face the front at all times.' He walked through the ranks checking their stance and posture. 'Now I'm going to bring you to attention, and I do that by shouting, "Parade! Parade. Shun!" And on that command this is what you do.' Sarah ran it over in her head as Ben was speaking. 'Force both hands down your back until they are rigid, head up, eyes looking over the head of the person in front. Next . . . hands to the side, thumbs in line with the seams of your trousers, bring left foot to right, heels together, toes out . . .'

Ben repeated it slowly, twice. 'Everybody got that?' They all said yes. 'We'll find out then, shall we? Parade! Par-AAAAAAAADE! SHUN!' Ben roared.

He waited a full minute and then shook his head. 'Be grateful the sergeant major isn't here. That . . . was an unmitigated disaster.'

Sarah looked around her. No one was in line any more. On Ben's first yell Maggie had given a small scream and leaped to the side. Phil had brought in his right foot instead of his left, as had many others, and she herself hadn't moved at all. The only person who seemed to have coped was David.

'Perhaps we should master the stand at ease first before moving on to something difficult?' suggested one of the cadets. 'Like, say, we could stand about at ease for the next hour?'

'Do you have to shout quite so loudly?' asked Maggie, rubbing her ears.

'That wasn't loud, dear,' replied Ben. 'Wait until you're on a parade ground. Some of the older drill instructors can shatter glass on passing aeroplanes.'

By the end of the night, they had achieved what Ben called an 'almost passable' come to attention. He looked at his watch. 'Time to get the kit off.'

As David opened his mouth, Sarah slapped her hand across it. 'Don't even think it,' she said.

Cal was getting dressed up. Ready for the big day. Check the mirror. It was superb this one, absolutely excellent. Tie needed adjusting though. The knot was too neat, slip it a little to one side . . . like so . . . exactly . . . Studied the reflection carefully. Yes . . . that would do . . .

A master of disguise . . .

10 Incident two – Altminster

Perhaps it was the silence, Sarah thought, as she closed her eyes and breathed in deeply. There was something terribly moving about the school Remembrance Day service. She was standing at the back of the school hall on Friday waiting for eleven o'clock, the time scheduled for their own service to begin. The whole school had been assembled, from the first year pupils sitting quietly in the front rows, right through to the seniors like herself, who were standing at the back, helping out with ushering and organisation.

Sarah thought of her gran's older brothers, the two great-uncles whom she had never met, never known. She thought of the children and grandchildren they might have had. The silence in the hall was absolute; it had fallen when the Head had said a few words asking people to reflect quietly within themselves as the eleventh hour approached.

As the hands on the large wooden clock above the stage approached the hour, the Head stood up and signalled to the music teacher. A third year pupil walked to the front of the stage and put a bugle to his lips. He began to play the *Last Post*.

Sarah felt tears standing in her eyes. And as the last note sounded, there was a deep sigh from all around her.

Then the pupils chosen to do the readings came forward and spoke in turn. A first year boy began, his unbroken voice making the words more poignant. '*Age shall not weary them, nor the years condemn . . .*' He paused at that point and stood back.

Each pupil did their reading; an extract from a book, a diary entry from the pages of a notebook found in a front-line trench, a love letter from a sweetheart and then the poem which Phil had chosen. The perfect poem, she had agreed, when he had told her of his choice. A poem to end wars, he had said. Reading it through with him had helped her understand his attitude to war – his own search for pacifism.

'Reconciliation' by Siegfried Sassoon

When you are standing at your hero's grave,
Or near some homeless village where he died,
Remember, through your heart's rekindling pride,
The German soldiers who were loyal and brave.
Men fought like brutes; and hideous things were done;
And you have nourished hatred, harsh and blind.
But in that Golgotha perhaps you'll find
The mothers of the men who killed your son.

Finally the same first year pupil completed his lines of verse: '*At the going down of the sun, and in the morning We will remember them . . .*'

Watching the television programme of the service at the Cenotaph in London with Gran on Sunday, Sarah felt the same drawing on her emotions. The veterans marched past, medals shining, some very old and frail but still determined to turn-out. Their presence made another facet in the whole spectacle – the uniforms, impeccably pressed, the bright colour of the standards, the black clothes of the guests of honour, the blood red of the poppies.

Gran took her hanky from her sleeve and wiped her eyes.

'Why do you watch it if it makes you sad?' asked Sarah.

Her gran thought for a bit. 'I suppose it also makes me feel good,' she said eventually. 'It's when I say goodbye to them,' she went on. 'I never got to say goodbye at the time.' She smiled at Sarah. 'And then I can be content for the rest of the year.'

On a sudden impulse Sarah took her bike from the garden shed and pedalled furiously up through the quiet streets of the town. Would she be on time? She was aiming for a particular spot. A viewpoint where she would be able to see Longheath's own service. It was a place where her dad and mum had taken her as a child to watch the Gala Day processions in the summer. There was an ornamental bench at the end of a wide crescent of Victorian villas which stood looking regally down on the museum, art gallery and city square. She propped her bike against a tree, hurriedly jumped up on the seat and scanned the streets below. There were people gathered round the war memorial. It was cold, and the wind was shuffling some autumn leaves around the open spaces. She was sure she could pick out Mr Eliott, and a few other people she knew, as they waited quietly with heads bent.

She heard the bagpipes first. They were playing *The Flowers of the Forest*. The sobbing note of the pipes called out in sadness to the grey skies above. The trudge of the marching feet was the only other noise to be heard, and with no accompaniment, the lament for the lost youth slain in battle made a heartbreaking sound across the empty city streets.

Sarah raised her hand to her throat as the column came into view. She heard the senior cadet's shout as he brought his line to a halt.

'Par-AAADE! Parade! Halt!'

They turned in unison, a perfect formation, line after line stretching down the road.

'Present arms!'

The wreaths were laid and the words said, and a lone piper played a pibroch to close the ceremony. Then the drums crashed out, the CO took the salute and, paced to their resonant boom, the parade saluted and turned. The tartan kilts swung, dark green squares crossed with red and yellow, as they marched off down the road.

And suddenly Sarah understood *exactly* why Harry and Bob, Gran's two older brothers, and every other boy in the village, had run out and joined them. She would have done it herself. It occurred to her that one of Gran's sadnesses must be that she herself had not gone with them. She imagined the little girl in the white pinafore standing in the dusty street watching them march away, crying inconsolably because she had been left behind.

Sarah experienced a further insight, and was frightened by its knowledge. She knew now why Phil thought it was dangerous. The call that kind of show made upon you. Deep in your psyche it aroused an emotion which demanded a response. It sang out to her, and she knew that, if asked, she would go, right now, this minute . . . blood stirred, heart flying, proud of her country, its music and its fighting men.

Sarah was gone quite a long time so that it was getting dark as she pedalled slowly back into her own driveway. She noticed her dad's car wasn't there. She checked the time on her watch. It was too early for him to be taking Gran home – she normally stayed for Sunday dinner before leaving. In fact, usually Dad made Sunday dinner. Where had he gone off to?

She returned her bike to the shed and went in the back door. Her mother was at the kitchen sink preparing vegetables.

'Oh there you are,' she said. 'Give me a hand here, pet, will you?'

'Sure.' She pulled open the cutlery drawer and began to pick up knives and forks. 'Where's Dad disappeared to?'

Her mum placed the peeler down carefully on the worktop. She spoke very slowly. 'He got a call out. A real bad one. Across the border down at Altminster. They were bringing units in from all over. Two bombs went off at the Remembrance Day service. Right among the crowds. A wee boy, who was waiting to lay down his poppies on the tomb of the Unknown Soldier, was killed, and two old folks very seriously injured.'

'My God,' said Sarah.

Her mum shook her head. 'It's awful, I know. They think it might be connected to the other explosion at Crosston.'

Sarah tidied up the kitchen while her mother gave her gran a lift home. Her gran had hardly eaten any dinner. She'd been very upset at the news of the death of the child.

There are crazies out there, thought Sarah. It must be some nutter with a warped mind who goes about harming innocent people. She hoped the police would trace them soon. They must surely have some information to go on. Her mum had said these explosions were linked to the bomb at Crosston. But how?

11 Watch and shoot!

Early on Monday morning, Maxwell, one of the Army's chief intelligence officers, and his deputy helicoptered into the military base a few kilometres west of Newcastle. They listened carefully as the police superintendent briefed them on all the details of the two incidents. 'Definitely the same operator,' said the superintendent. 'Pieces of the timing mechanism found after the explosion have the same origin. The same materials used, similar targets. And also this . . . It was phoned into the number we gave to the press for anyone with information to ring.'

He flicked the switch on a tape recorder, and a curious high-pitched voice began to speak. '*Remember* . . . *Remember* . . . I don't want you to forget me . . . Number one made me cross . . .' There was a short laugh. '*Very* cross indeed. Number two. A better clue. One . . . Two . . . Three . . .' There was a pause, and a squeaky sing-song voice chanted. '*Remember . . . Remember . . .*'

Then the voice was cut off as the superintendent switched the machine off. He looked at the two men seated opposite him. 'We thought it was the fifth . . . to do with Houses of Parliament. Shall I run it again?' he queried.

Maxwell shook his head. 'Not at the moment, thanks.' He looked at his deputy. 'Using an electronic voice disguiser?'

His deputy nodded. Maxwell turned back to the police officer. 'Background noise?'

'Motorway traffic,' said the policeman. 'And the next answer is no, nowhere identifiable. But . . . we think the "cross" is Crosston. A wild guess, perhaps . . .'

'No,' Maxwell interrupted him. 'No, I think you're right there. The whole thing is full of references and veiled comments.'

'He's going to strike again,' said Maxwell's deputy. The policeman raised an eyebrow. 'Follow the clues, he told us.'

'"One . . . Two . . . Three . . ."'

'Yes,' said Maxwell, 'and the next time it will probably be *three* bombs. He's playing a game.' Maxwell got up from his chair and crossed to the wall map. 'Where are the bomb locations from here?'

'Altminster is about ninety kilometres north, on this side of the border. Crosston, much further away, up in the Lothians.' The superintendent pointed them out on the map.

Maxwell chewed his lip. 'No connection between them?'

The policeman shook his head. 'None that we can see. We've checked every possible angle. Every demographic detail, past history, biographies of famous residents, the lot.' He raised his shoulders and let them drop again. 'They appear to have nothing in common.'

'I want an intelligence check run with every known subversive contact we have,' Maxwell said. 'Top priority. Every grass, snooper, double agent, disaffected patriot on the list. Anyone with a habit, who's known to the security service and who is inside at the moment, stop the supply. Whoever the bomber is, he's off the wall, but he's got materials. Where did he get them? I want a fix on this.'

Maxwell returned to the table and glanced briefly through the notes which he had been given on arrival at the base. 'We'll do the check thoroughly, although it may be wasting time.' He took the file and slipped it into his briefcase, and then spoke to his deputy. 'I think we both know it's "another agency".'

The deputy nodded his head. Maxwell turned to the superintendent. 'It's a term used to describe someone acting outside the remit of the known and recognised terrorist groups.' He rubbed his forehead with his forefinger. 'I think what we are dealing with here is that most dangerous of species. The solitary agent. A single operator. Similar to the one who got past the Shin Bet, Israel's crack security service, and assassinated Prime Minister Rabin. As their own former chief stated, "There is no solution for the man who decides to act alone."'

On Tuesday, at the third Army introduction night, Ben was of the same opinion. 'All the older officers I know in the regulars are saying that it must be a lone nutter,' he told Sarah as they waited for the others to arrive. The hall was unnaturally quiet, the cadets subdued. Most of them had been on parade in Longheath on Sunday and felt that they could easily have been the target instead of Altminster. 'It's thought that the main known organisations would be falling over themselves to claim responsibility,' Ben continued. 'They crave publicity. It's one of the reasons they do it. There's no point in murdering innocent civilians without claiming the glory.'

'Glory,' repeated Sarah. 'It wasn't a very glorious thing to do.'

'Well a lot of them truly believe they are acting for their country,' said Ben.

Sarah looked at him in surprise. These were the sentiments which Phil had expressed. It hadn't occurred to her that Ben would think along the same lines. 'So you admire them for that?'

'No,' said Ben slowly. 'I certainly don't admire anyone who chooses a soft target, but I try to understand the reason behind the forming of nationalist groups. If you read the history of the Middle East or Ireland then you can see there are two sides to the story. It is understandable that people get all fired up for one side or the other. In fact, it's similar in the Army. You are proud to belong, to be prepared to serve your country.'

Sarah hadn't imagined that Ben recognised that particular aspect of the training. 'But that doesn't make it right to plant bombs,' she persisted.

'Of course it's not right,' said Ben. 'And obviously underground movements attract those with criminal motives. They are revenging personal grievances, drug-pushing, making money through protection rackets. And I believe the no-holds-barred type of conflict is morally wrong.'

'But you don't think all killing is wrong?' asked Sarah.

'No, I don't. I would have shot the bomber at

Altminster on sight.' He looked up as Phil and David came walking towards them. 'And by coincidence tonight's topic is weapon skills.' He turned quickly as the boys approached and picked up a rifle which was lying on the table. He made as if to throw it at Phil. Phil reached up quickly with both hands. 'Good,' said Ben. 'Quick reflexes.'

'I saw it as a rugby ball,' said Phil at once. 'Not a gun.'

'Well tonight we're going to find out how good a shot you are.'

Phil groaned, and Maggie, who had just joined them said, 'It's going to be noisy isn't it? Guns go bang. I feel a headache coming on.'

'Guns don't go bang actually,' laughed Ben. 'But you'll be wearing earplugs anyway. We'll have to wait our turn for the range. There's a special instructor and he can only take four at a time.' He looked at his watch. 'I think we're the third group in. We should be ready to go in half an hour or so.'

'Oh, good,' said Maggie, 'half an hour with nothing to do.' She looked at Ben. 'Wrong thing to say?'

'Correct,' said Ben. 'In the Army there is never nothing to do. I've got information sheets for you all which give details about the away day which will be this weekend. Please fill in the return slip at the bottom and give it to me before you leave, so that I know if and when I'm picking you up. And then we are going to do a little self-development exercise with you.'

Maggie swiftly side-stepped and then moved back so that she was no longer at the front. 'Super,' she said. 'I take it we're all agreed that David's first?'

Sarah and Phil nodded vigorously.

'This one's painless,' said Ben.

'That'll be a first,' murmured Phil.

'It's all to do with building confidence,' said Ben. He quickly arranged a few rows of chairs and waved over some of the other groups as he was speaking. 'The rest of you sit down,' he indicated the seats in front of them, 'while David stands out at the front facing you. Now the Army needs leaders with self-assurance, who are able to think on their feet, take charge at a moment's notice, and reassure and inspire their team by their ability to perform instantaneously.' He paused. 'I'm sure we have one in David. David is now going to speak to us for two minutes.'

'I am?' said David.

'You are,' said Ben firmly, and he took a seat right at the front.

'On what?' asked David.

'Oh, anything.' Ben waved his hands in the air. 'Your life as a ballet dancer.'

There were hoots of laughter from the audience.

'But . . .'

'Starting now,' said Ben pointing to his watch. 'In the Army you must perform when ordered.'

'Oh . . . right. Ummm . . .' David glanced around him desperately. 'Right . . . OK.' He grinned. 'I'm here to address you all today on the subject of my chosen career as a member of the Royal Ballet Company. However . . . before we begin, I would like to draw your attention to a few necessary safety regulations. May I first of all point out to you the fire exits. They are situated at each end of the hall with a further third door in the middle. In the event of a fire the procedure is as follows . . .'

'Well done, David,' exclaimed Ben, exactly at the end of the two minutes as David wound up his instructions on what the audience should do in the event of a fire in the building.

Maggie and Sarah began to applaud enthusiastically.

'He was cheating,' said Phil.

'No I wasn't.'

'You were. I could see you reading every word from the fire notice beside you on the wall.'

'So?' said David. 'Initiative, old son. That's what that's called.'

As they waited to go into the firing-range Sarah thought about David. She felt that he had changed over the last two weeks of the Army nights. His performance on the assault course, last week's kit inspection, and tonight . . . his confidence was growing. He was speaking out now with his own opinions, rather than as previously, when he always made the jokes and left the serious stuff to Phil. And Phil had altered, too. He was less uptight, he was beginning to enjoy himself. He still had arguments with Ben, but he was more inclined to hear out the other point of view.

The target practice was another revelation. But this time it was to do with herself. Once on the firing-range Sarah found the fit of the gun on her shoulder quite comfortable, where she had thought it would be heavy and awkward. She also discovered that she enjoyed the whole exercise. The officer in charge gave them a serious preliminary talk on the strict rules for indoor firing. 'Remember safety is paramount,' he warned them. 'For yourself and for others.'

There were four targets – one each – and they lined up and listened as the officer gave instructions on how to load and fire. He emphasised again that safety was the prime consideration, and that every action taken had to be carefully checked. On manoeuvres they would remove their beret and put the rounds in it. Then the rounds are loaded into the magazine and the magazine clicked into place on the rifle. On the command 'make ready' the cocking handle is pulled back and then released to prepare to fire.

The officer came to each one of them, checked their weapon and explained how to centre the cross hairs, and how to avoid tipping the rifle to one side. 'If you cant the rifle, the shot will not go where you think you've placed it,' he told them. He went back down the line to the end. 'Think about your breathing. If you breathe in and out as normal then the weapon will rise and fall. Breathe in. Hold. Fire. That's the way. OK? Last instruction: don't snatch at the trigger. He went back down the line and stood at the end. Then he gave the commands loud and distinct.

'Make ready.

'Targets will fall when hit.

'Watch and shoot! Watch and shoot!'

Afterwards they were given their scorecards to keep.

'Right in the middle,' said Maggie. 'I'm an ace shot.'

'Actually, no,' said Ben. 'You've only got one on the target, the rest have gone wide. Probably your breathing was irregular. So that means you're erratic. Ideally you should be able to balance a small coin steadily on the muzzle just before you fire.' He looked at the rest. 'Sarah,' he said. 'You're a good shot. See,' he pointed to Sarah's card.

'It's better to have a small grouping, close together, like that. It means your aim is more true. Then it's just a case of adjusting so that you hit centre.'

Sarah looked at her card. A small circle of holes had been driven through the target's chest. She had a close grouping.

'Good marksmanship,' said Ben.

'Let me see your card,' Sarah asked Phil.

Very reluctantly he took it out of his pocket.

His was almost identical to hers. A series of bullet holes close to the heart of the target.

'You've gone off the orientation course now, haven't you?' Sarah asked. They were walking once again along the main road to the bus stop. Phil had taken her arm as soon as they came out of the drill hall, and Sarah found that she really didn't mind the assured way that he now did this. She enjoyed walking close to him and chatting, the companionship, the comforting feel of him beside her. And she knew him well enough now to know that he was upset.

'It was hearing the instructor saying, "Targets will fall when hit",' said Phil, 'and seeing the bullet holes through the figure drawing.' He pulled his scorecard from his pocket and looked at it again. Then with a sudden violent movement he tore it up.

What a difference in their attitudes, thought Sarah. She knew that she would keep her own card, show it to her parents and tell Gran at the weekend that Ben thought she was a crack shot.

'You forget that one day it will be real ammunition, a real person,' said Phil.

'No,' said Sarah slowly. 'I don't forget. I hope that it won't be needed, but I accept the fact that it might be, and I do believe in the training.'

'Are you thinking of Altminster?' Phil asked her.

'I suppose so. It was a horrible thing to happen on Remembrance Day. My gran was terribly upset.'

'I know. I kept thinking about the little kid, and my own wee sister.'

Sarah faced him. 'Yet, despite that, you would still keep to your pacifist principles?'

Phil smiled grimly. 'Isn't that what you are meant to do with principles? Stick to them?'

'Peace at any price?' Sarah repeated Mr Eliott's words. 'I don't know. It didn't work with Hitler.' She looked at him anxiously. 'You'll still come on the away day?'

'Oh yes.' He pulled her closer against him. 'I don't ever start something and not see it through.'

12 Feel good – Perform

'Three miles done and two to go . . .' sang out the drill sergeant.

'Fifteen men, we're runnin' slow . . .' the running men chanted in reply.

'Runnin' slow. You'd better fly . . .' yelled the sergeant jogging alongside them.

'We'll keep on a-runnin' till we die . . .' the answer chorused back.

Sarah, with the group of girls waiting in their three ranks further down the circuit, heard them long before they saw them. The dull thunder of the boots against the hard track, all in rhythm, the singing voices, the jingle of the equipment they carried. Sarah felt suppressed tension build inside her.

'I hope we can keep up with them when they get here,' said Maggie, nervously tucking a strand of hair behind her ear.

'We ought to,' said Sarah. 'They've already run two thirds of the course. We're only joining in the last couple of miles.' She broke off. 'Look.'

The section of men came over the top of the hill and down the slope on the other side, dust rising at their feet, louder and louder as they approached.

'Here we come, we're doin' fine . . .'

'Fifteen soldiers all in line . . .'

A rush of excitement surged through Sarah and she began, with a few others, to hop about at the side of the road.

'Hold it!' bellowed their sergeant. 'Wait for it . . . ! Wait for it . . . ! NOW! GO! GO! GO!'

The boys reached them and ran past in tight formation whooping and cheering, and the girls fell in behind.

Sarah soon discovered that it wasn't easy to keep the pace they had set, not wearing full combat gear and carrying a rifle. Better than it might have been though. Ben had told them earlier that on competitive runs their webbing would be weighted with sand and checked before and after. 'It is to do with fitness,' he had said. 'Fitness means being able to complete a task. *Military* fitness means you do a run then follow it with some testing exercises. It is the backbone of Army training. You undertake a march, then a shoot, to make you able to cope with battle conditions.'

'So . . . that's the plan for today, is it?' Maggie had asked him. 'We run until we are exhausted, and then go straight on to an assault course without stopping.'

Ben had smiled. 'What did you expect for the away day? The seaside? Sandcastles?'

Maggie had smiled in return. 'Not really,' she had sighed.

Maggie turned to Sarah who was running beside her. 'I'll have to drop back,' she gasped. 'You go on.'

Sarah slowed a little to stay beside her friend. 'Don't worry. They have to wait for us before they begin the obstacle race. We're supposed to work as a team on that one.' She glanced up as a helicopter chuntered low over their heads. 'That looks like our reception committee getting ready to harass us.'

'I can't believe it,' moaned Maggie. 'It's bad enough having to complete one of these outdoor courses without having whirlybirds swooping about chucking flares and making fake attacks.'

Sarah laughed. 'It's to give it some authenticity. We're supposed to fall flat on the ground if they come near us. I think it should be quite exciting.'

'I'm beginning to realise that your idea of what is exciting is vastly different from mine,' panted Maggie. 'I noticed you were extremely interested in how they were preparing the mock-up wounded earlier on.'

'It was fascinating.'

'It was disgusting!' exclaimed Maggie. 'Splodgy bits of flesh hanging off bodies, and eye sockets blacked out.'

'It's to simulate the shock of battle,' said Sarah. 'We have to get used to grim conditions. You wouldn't be any help whatsoever to a wounded comrade if you sick up at the sight of a torn toenail. Ben said the Welsh Guards suffered horrific injuries in the Falklands, and it was their training and courage which helped to pull them through.'

'Well, if I trip over any wounded personnel on the ground, I'm not examining them too closely,' said Maggie.

'David's carrying the radio for our team,' said Sarah. 'It's up to him to arrange medical help. I just hope we don't get lost or that we are so slow the follow-up platoon catch up with us.'

Maggie grinned suddenly. 'Oh, I don't know. I was chatting to some of the boys in E Company. I found them quite friendly.'

Sarah laughed. 'Fraternising with the enemy is treason.' She looked up again as the helicopter came across once more. 'Nearly there.'

Ben talked them through the course briefly a second time, and then shook their hands solemnly. 'Take care in the minefield at the end,' he said.

'Minefield?' repeated Maggie. 'I'm out of here!'

'It's only trays of coloured paint concealed in the long grass. At the end of the course you will have points deducted for the amount splashed on your uniform,' said Ben. 'Remember, all obstacles are negotiable. That means they can be climbed over or crawled under . . .' He glanced at Maggie. 'Or through.'

They shouldered their bergens, apart from David who was excused carrying the Army rucksack as he had the radio. Sarah could see that he was rather proud of this responsibility. He had spent some time mastering the call signs and studying his copy of the forces alphabet code.

'Look at this backpack,' grumbled Maggie. 'Where am I supposed to put my make-up bag and mirror? There's no room.'

'No make-up. No jewellery,' said Ben. 'Now let's progress to the FEBA.'

'Forward Edge of Battle Area,' said David at once.

They lined up and Ben checked their 'Time Out,' and gave them their maps and instructions. 'There are emergency rendez-vouz points marked "RVS" on your map in case of injury. And the route is basically circular, so I'll be waiting here to check your "Time In".'

Ahead of them they could see a row of logs set over an artificial pond of mud, various large pieces of piping beyond that and, in the far distance, scramble nets were draped down an impossibly high wooden fence. Above them the chopper buzzed noisily.

'Oh, God,' said Maggie.

'Give me your pack,' Phil said to her, as soon as they set off. Sarah looked at him questioningly. 'We're being timed as a unit,' he explained. 'It's what we'd do in the field, in adverse circumstances.'

'Suits me,' said Maggie.

David put out his hand for Sarah's, but she shook her head and pulled out her copy of the field orders. '"Negotiate every obstacle and collect numbered metal disc. Call back to HQ at each stage, and also radio the location of any casualties needing urgent transportation out."' She shoved the notes back in her pocket. 'Let's go.'

Character building. Sarah laughed out loud as this phrase of Ben's popped into her head about half an hour later. Her left foot had caught in the net on the way over the fence and she was hanging almost upside down, yelling at the others to come back and help her.

'Hang on,' said Phil clambering back up beside her. He

supported her shoulders as she disentangled her ankle.

Very romantic, thought Sarah. She was soaked in perspiration and covered in mud.

'Just the trek across open ground and then the minefield,' Phil told her encouragingly.

They both looked up at the sky. The helicopter was hovering over the rocky heathland in front of them.

'Which is what that chopper's waiting for I suppose,' said Sarah.

'Let's split up and run for it,' suggested David. 'They can't delay all of us simultaneously.'

They lined up together.

'On my word,' said Phil, 'we scatter and run.' He winked at Sarah. 'Ready?' She nodded and gripped her rifle. 'NOW!'

Immediately the open area came under simulated fire. The flash of the flares, the noise of the swirling rotor blades directly above, and the rough terrain made them stumble and fall. The engine filled their heads with sound as the machine thundered overhead. It had gone after Phil to begin with, but he had immediately flung himself flat out and lay still. Sarah saw it swing round and come towards her. She bent low and kept running, then saw a foxhole a little way off and dived for cover. To find . . . as she rolled into the soft earth at the bottom . . . that it was already occupied. There was a soldier sitting there quietly reading a book. He took off his glasses, put them away carefully, and then let out a tremendous yell.

'Aaaaarghhhhhh! I'm wounded!'

'Where?'

'Everywhere.'

'Oh come on,' said Sarah, 'let me know the details quickly. We're being timed on this.'

'Give us a snog and I'll tell you.'

Sarah lifted her gun. 'I think I'll shoot you to put you out of your misery.'

'Severe internal,' he said at once. 'You can't deal with it yourself. Call HQ and tell them you need a stretcher rescue party and get me case-vaced out.'

Remembering the instruction about using the field-dressing to relieve pain, Sarah tore the dog tag string and stuck a 'morphine given' sticker on his forehead. 'There,' she told him cheerfully. 'That's probably got a street value of about sixty quid. So be happy until a chopper picks you up.'

He grabbed her wrist. 'Hey gorgeous. See you in the mess afterwards?'

'Let go,' she ordered him, 'or I'll radio a wrong rescue position back to base and E Company will capture you. They've never read the rule book, I heard they can be rough.'

He dropped her arm and grinned at her. 'Bit of advice,' he said seriously. 'I ran this course last year. Bear left on the minefield.'

'Thanks.'

'Now do I get a snog?'

Sarah laughed and ran off to catch up the rest.

Later in the showers Maggie rummaged around in her holdall. 'I've forgotten my curling tongs!' Sarah laughed. 'Well it's all right for you,' said Maggie. 'Your hair is long enough to tie back.' Maggie took out a small mirror and examined herself. 'Look at my face,' she shrieked. 'It's not just bright red. It's purple in places!'

Sarah peered at herself in the small mirror. 'Mine's not just purple in places – it's puce all over!' She dragged Maggie by her arm. 'Let's get to the mess. I'm starving.'

'If these are Army rations then I'm all for it,' said David as they ate dinner in the canteen.

Ben brought his plate and sat beside them. 'I heard you four performed really well.'

'Performed,' said Phil. 'Now that's an interesting word.'

'Oh be quiet, Phil Jarvis,' said Sarah. 'I saw your face earlier; you were enjoying yourself out there.'

'So were you,' said Maggie.

'Yes, I was,' Sarah admitted. 'I thought it was brilliant.'

'Brilliant?' repeated Phil.

'You've got a thing about language, haven't you Phil?' said Ben.

'It's interesting the way it's used by the military,' said Phil. 'You steal all the exciting words. It makes combat sound glamorous. The jargon in the field, the names for things, it creates a particular effect. For instance, in the Gulf War the enemy missiles were known as "Scuds" whereas ours were called "Patriots".'

'I'd rather have a Patriot weapon than a Scud,' said David.

'Exactly,' said Phil.

'So what's your point?' asked Ben.

'It's just that all this,' Phil waved his hand around in the air, 'is very gung-ho. And possibly deliberately designed that way, so that soldiers who have taken part can be easily led into fighting a war.'

'Except, Phil . . .' said Sarah putting her hand on his sleeve. He turned to look at her, and she stared at him seriously. '. . . in the Army the training isn't totally about war. It is also about peace.'

13 Final Command Task

Cal was happy. The most happy for a long time. The papers were full of pictures and exciting words. 'Dangerous lunatic.' That was a good phrase. It sounded important and special. It mentioned the telephone call. That was good too. That they had known something . . . enough to make them twitchy . . . and to feel stupid later. It could be done again. Have them scurrying around frantically. Give more clues, not too many, but some, so that they would realise afterwards they could have worked it out if they'd been smart enough. But not to do it by phone . . . mustn't use it again. They were able to carry out a location check now in seconds . . . Cal looked at the newspapers again . . .

* * *

'Command Task tonight,' said Ben the following Tuesday evening. 'But before we begin can I say that it's been an . . . interesting experience leading your group, and I hope that you'll all decide to do the selection weekend. I need names fairly soon.' He looked round at them. 'I found the last few weeks good fun, I've really enjoyed them.'

'So have I, actually,' said Phil. Sarah looked at him in surprise. 'Well I have. I'm not too proud to admit that.'

'Yeah, it was good,' agreed David.

Sarah nodded.

'Emmm . . . would have to clarify your definition of "fun", Ben,' said Maggie. 'Mine runs along the lines of films, parties, music, receiving expensive presents . . . you know, all those trivial things which make life more bearable.' Then she smiled at him. 'Don't look so upset. I *did* enjoy myself . . . from time to time,' she added under her breath.

Ben returned the smile. 'Good. Now gather your chairs round one of the tables and I'll give you a problem to work out. Pen and paper might help.' He put some on the table. 'Remember there is no right or wrong answer. In fact, there may not be any solution at all. This is known as a Command Task.'

'So who is in command?' asked Maggie.

'You can decide that yourself, or work out the problem

together.' He looked at them. 'Do you think it is always necessary to have someone in command?'

'No,' said Maggie.

'Yes,' said Phil and Sarah together.

David shrugged. 'Depends. What is it?'

'Here are the details,' said Ben. 'You are a patrol returning from behind enemy lines with information which is of vital importance. The orders are to get the information back to HQ as soon as possible. Your radio is malfunctioning; you can receive messages from base, but are unable to transmit any. You are crossing No-Man's-Land. The enemy is closing up behind you, and as you move across the terrain you meet an obstacle.'

'Which is?' asked Sarah.

'A straight-up wall of solid ice, ten metres high.'

The four friends looked at each other.

'Ummm,' said Maggie.

'We wouldn't have ice-axes and crampons in our bergens by any chance?' David asked hopefully.

'You would not,' said Ben.

'A rope?'

'Nope.'

'Ten metres high?' said Phil.

'Ten metres,' repeated Ben. 'Like a sheet of glass.'

'Oh dear,' said Maggie. 'Looks like we'll just have to

give up and go to the bar.'

'You are in a forward position,' said Ben, 'and beginning to come under enemy fire.'

'How long is the wall?' asked Sarah.

'Very long.'

'Longer than the Great Wall of China?'

Ben nodded.

'Do we have any equipment other than a duff radio?' asked Phil.

Ben shook his head.

'See, this is where a hairdryer would come in handy,' said Maggie. 'You all laughed at me on the away day because I complained about the lack of facilities. When I asked if those wee pockets in the rucksacks had been designed to hold nail varnish or curling tongs, I was mocked and made fun of. Now, if I had been allowed my travel hairdryer, you would all be *begging* for a loan of it to blast a hole in that wall.'

The rest of them turned and looked at her.

'Shut up, Maggie,' said David.

'Right,' said Maggie huffily. 'I will. You can sort this out by yourselves. I'm going to negotiate terms of surrender with the enemy.'

'The terrain,' said Sarah. 'Can you describe it please?'

'It is absolutely barren,' said Ben. 'Oh, no, wait a

second. What's that lying on the ground over there?'

'A fifteen-metre ladder?' suggested David.

'A seven-and-a-half-metre telegraph pole,' said Ben.

'A *seven-and-a-half-metre* telegraph pole?' said Sarah. She picked up a piece of paper and a pen, and drew the wall with the telegraph pole leaning against it. Her friends looked over her shoulder.

'We lean the telegraph pole against the wall,' said Sarah slowly, 'and then one person climbs up . . .'

'And they still don't reach the top of the wall,' said David. 'Because in order to lean the telegraph pole against the wall at an angle you'd lose about half a metre in height. It's all to do with Pythagoras and his right-angled whatsit.' He scribbled on the paper. 'You can work it out mathematically . . . A metre-and-a-half stretch to allow us to climb up reaches to . . . say, seven metres. So with you reaching to full height Phil, we're still short.'

'What if a second soldier comes behind,' said Sarah, 'and climbs on the first person's shoulders?' She looked at Ben. 'Would he reach the top of the wall?'

'He . . . or she . . . would,' said Ben.

'Then,' said David, 'the next one comes up, and the next. When three are at the top, they reach down and haul the last soldier over.'

'No,' said Ben. 'The pole won't stay in place by itself.

The wall is too slippy. Also, may I remind you that HQ *need* that information. Many lives depend on it.'

They all puzzled over the sheet of paper for a few minutes, turning it this way and that and trying to work out complicated permutations with each different soldier.

'I suppose we could all strip off, tie our clothes together to make a rope and haul the last person up with it,' said David.

'You are now receiving a radio message from HQ,' said Ben.

'Oh good,' said Maggie.

'I don't think it is,' said Sarah, watching Ben's face.

'Heavy artillery has moved up behind you and is now preparing to fire.'

'Quick! Clothes off!' shouted David.

'You are now under fire.'

David jumped up, dragged off his jacket and began unbuckling the belt of his trousers.

'Sit down, you fool,' said Maggie, pushing him back into his seat.

Ben looked at his watch. 'In thirty seconds the enemy will score a direct hit on your present position.'

'Then there is no solution,' said Sarah throwing the pen on to the table. She looked at Ben. 'That's it, isn't it? There was no solution.'

'Is that what you're telling me?' he asked.

'Looks like it,' said David.

Maggie nodded.

'Phil?'

Phil spoke slowly. 'There is one solution,' he said. He looked round at his friends. 'You leave someone behind.'

'They'll get killed,' said David.

Phil shrugged. 'It's a solution,' he said. 'We are carrying urgent information. Maybe it has a direct bearing on where we are.'

'So who gets left behind?' asked Maggie.

Phil stared directly at Ben. 'That's why you need someone in command,' he said.

'Phil, I'm appointing you in command,' said Ben. 'Tell me what action you would take.'

'I'd climb the pole first because I'm the tallest and the strongest. Then I'd punt two others over.'

'Name them and say why you chose them,' said Ben.

Phil heaved a sigh. 'Maggie first, she's the lightest and she'd be over quick. Then David, because I need his strength to haul me up.'

Sarah gasped. 'You can't make me stay in No-Man's-Land,' she said. 'I'm almost as tall as you. I can help them over too.'

'Yes,' said Phil, 'but you're not as strong. And, anyway, I'm the commander. There might be problems on the other side which I would have to deal with. I have to go.'

'I can't believe this,' said Sarah. She turned to the other two. 'He's leaving me behind.'

'Quite right too,' said Maggie. 'You were only a liability anyway.'

'Yeah,' said David. 'In any case, you should have done the decent thing and volunteered.'

'Ben,' Sarah appealed to him. 'Am I to be left behind?'

'Ask the commander,' Ben advised her. 'It's his decision.'

'The orders were to get the information back to HQ,' said Phil stubbornly. 'It said nothing about preserving the life of the soldiers. I was following the orders.'

'Ha!' said Sarah in mock derision. 'How many people throughout history have used that particular excuse? "I was only following orders."'

'Exactly,' said Phil miserably. 'That's the bit I don't like about all of this.'

Sarah appealed to Ben. 'Is that the solution?'

'It is *a* solution,' said Ben.

'I would be killed,' said Sarah.

Ben regarded her seriously. 'Very likely,' he said.

At lunchtime the next day, still feeling uncomfortable

about the previous night, Phil went in search of Sarah. He found her in the computer lab.

'What are you up to in here?' he asked as he opened the door.

'Say again?' said Sarah, concentrating on the screen in front of her.

'Pardon?'

Sarah looked up at him. 'Sorry,' she smiled. 'What did you say?'

'Never mind what I said,' said Phil. 'You do realise that you are picking up Army slang?'

'What?'

'A moment ago, you used the expression "Say again?"'

Sarah stared at him for a second, trying to follow the conversation. Then she grinned up at him. 'Say again?' she said.

He grabbed her hair and pulled her head back not very gently. 'Owww!' she yelped. 'Sorry, I surrender. Truce. White Flag.'

'Even those are military terms,' said Phil letting her go. He dragged over a chair and sat down beside her.

'I'm not speaking to you anyway,' said Sarah tossing her head. 'You left me to my fate in No-Man's-Land.'

'Yes,' said Phil. 'I wanted to explain about that. You see the urgent information which I managed to deliver to HQ turned out to be the co-ordinates of the enemy position, so our artillery knocked them out immediately and you were rescued. Alive and well.'

'I don't believe you.'

'It's true,' said Phil. 'You got a medal for bravery actually,' he added.

'Rubbish.'

'No really,' Phil insisted. 'From the Queen. At Buckingham Palace in a special ceremony. It was in all the papers.'

Sarah turned from the computer and looked at him. 'Thank you, Phil,' she said quietly. 'It's a very nice story, and things like that do happen in wartime, but we both know that the reality could be a lot more nasty.'

He looked away. 'Yeah,' he said shortly.

She put her hand on his. 'I can accept it. Obviously I don't want to be the one who is left behind, but I can see how decisions like that must be taken.'

'Doesn't it put you off the whole Army thing?'

She shook her head.

He sighed heavily. 'It does me.'

'I guess we see it from different viewpoints then.'

'Opposites attract?' said Phil. He leaned over and peered at her computer screen. 'What *are* you doing?'

'Playing about,' she replied. 'I thought if I put in all the information about the two bomb explosions, they might possibly cross-reference.'

'In what way?'

'Oh, I don't know,' said Sarah wearily. She took her disc out and pressed the power switch. The screen went black, and she stared at it for a moment or two. 'My dad says that the information the paramedics had was that the two explosions were linked. And I know Ben believes that Army Intelligence think there is a connection. I thought that if I ran the information through the computer, something would show up. But it hasn't. There doesn't seem to be a pattern to it at all.'

14 Pattern repeat

'There's always a pattern,' said Maxwell. 'A reason for a place being chosen.'

'And if we knew where the next place was going to be, then we'd know what the reason was,' said his deputy wryly.

'I think we are being told.' Maxwell looked at the piece of paper lying in front of him. 'Or at least being given enough of a clue, so that when the third explosion occurs we'll feel very foolish that we didn't work it out.'

'Not only foolish,' said the deputy, 'but angry and frustrated. There's someone out there with deep resentment and a very sick mind.'

'Can you sense it too?' asked Maxwell. He lifted the sheet of paper with the message made of letters cut from newspapers and brought it close to his face. 'It makes me shudder when I think that the person who killed that child has recently touched this.'

His deputy looked at him, and then said briskly. 'Yes, quite . . . he's also very careful. Our labs couldn't pick up any prints from the paper. It was sent to a national newspaper and the envelope was postmarked Manchester. We're checking if there is any Manchester connection.' He reached over and clicked the switch on the OHP and a copy of Cal's warning message appeared large on the screen before them.

I'm Going to make You
work HarD for a LiviNg
abc
it's eLemEntaree
One two Three
3 x 3
dEfiniteLy
three [...]

Despite the fact that they already knew every character, they studied the words again. Was there something more contained in it than they had already worked out? Instinctively they felt that there was.

It was the same with the tape, thought Maxwell. He'd run it dozens of times . . . knew each phrase . . . each syllable off by heart. The taunting voice kept him awake at night. And now they had a second message. This time in writing. And they were getting nowhere. This guy is so cocky . . . full of himself. Maxwell could feel his annoyance rise, and he tried to fight it down. Becoming angry didn't help at all. He had to think straight. 'Run it past me again, John,' he said.

His deputy talked quietly, occasionally glancing at his notes lying on the table in front of him. 'If you try to follow the logic of this warning then . . . he is making us work hard, trying to solve this. Also, he probably watches them clearing up the mess on the television afterwards. So that fits the working hard for a living. He doesn't like authority, maybe there is some bitterness towards youth . . . perhaps his own childhood. We think this because of the soft targets and the tone of the messages, the rhymes . . . nursery rhymes . . .' The deputy's voice tailed off for a moment.

'What?' said Maxwell. 'You've thought of something?'

His deputy shook his head. 'No . . . it'll come back.' He went on. 'A. B. C. We're not sure about this . . . Something with letters, or a significant name. His own? The town's? Are they connected? We've got archivists searching through past records and news files. Hopefully they'll come up with something.' He exchanged a glance with Maxwell. 'We've always got to hope,' he said firmly. 'The most definite pattern at the moment is the "three". It will be the third time. We believe he'll use three bombs . . . There seems to be a third "three" mentioned here that we don't know about. Perhaps linked to the towns . . . or himself . . . We don't know.'

'And that's the crux of it, isn't it?' said Maxwell bitterly. 'We don't *know* anything. We're guessing all the time.'

'But we've been correct on a couple of things.'

'Correct,' agreed Maxwell, 'but too late.'

'Because we weren't called in until after,' his deputy spoke reassuringly. 'Now we've got something to work on, and a bit of time to do it.'

Maxwell spoke, thinking aloud. 'How much time do we have? He seems to favour the end of the week, though there's not been enough incidents to mark that as a definite. It can't be too soon, because he wanted to get this to us beforehand. How far in advance was the other warning? A day, a day and a half?'

'He'd allow for post getting held up . . . So . . .'

'Saturday,' said his deputy suddenly.

'Saturday?' repeated Maxwell.

The deputy stood up. 'Saturday's child,' he said, excitement in his voice. 'The rhyme . . . that's what clicked in my head earlier. You know the one, *"Monday's child is fair of face, Tuesday's child is full of grace . . ."* It goes on to *"Friday's child is loving and giving, Saturday's child . . ."*'

'"Works hard for a living,"' Maxwell finished for him. He stared at the screen. The grim words mocked him.

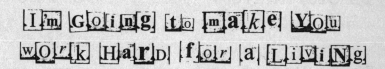

The killer was going to strike on Saturday. Was this now all they had to go on? Maxwell looked at the calendar. It was three days to the weekend.

'We need a break,' he said. 'A lucky break.'

15 Stalemate

'Here boy. Let's try this one.'

The mongrel dog walking on the road by the side of the old man stopped obediently.

'Smell anything?' old Sam asked, pointing at the rubbish bin in the lay-by. 'No?' He reached over and patted the dog's head affectionately. 'Let me have a wee look.'

The dog sat back on its haunches and watched its master rummaging among the rubbish. Old Sam mumbled away as he searched.

'Nothing much of any good in this one. Beer cans, empty bottles . . .' These wayside bins were filthy, didn't get emptied for months at a time. Sometimes you had to dig down into them before you found anything worthwhile. For decent food or clothes . . . best bet was the house bins.

It would amaze you what people threw out. Perfectly respectable goods. He had discovered an almost new suit one day. Not quite his size, that was true, but in mint condition nevertheless. And food! Well, they said folk were starving. Depends what you called starving. Half-eaten chickens, roast beef and all those carton take-aways that the youngsters bought. You only had to wait around the town centres at night. They flung them away with most of the contents in them. Still warm if you were quick enough.

'Nothing here,' he told the dog. 'No, wait.' Right at the bottom, well wrapped up, what was this? A bundle of something.

He reached in and pulled the package out. 'Aha, newspapers.' A whole batch of them.

It was becoming more difficult to find newspapers these days. All the new recycling bins at the supermarkets meant folks hardly ever threw them out now. Not like the old times. You could rely on getting newspapers by the bin, wrapped up neatly with a piece of string. String. That was another thing that was getting scarcer. He didn't know when he'd last seen a decent piece of string. The proper kind; thick, brown and unbreakable. He hauled the papers out, and stuffed them into his plastic carrier bags. They used that nylon tape now to tie up boxes. What good was that to anyone? You couldn't re-use it, couldn't even burn it. Not like these papers. He would burn them . . . eventually. Wrap himself up in them for a few nights first though. He would need them tonight. Soon be too cold to sleep out. In a few days he would have to head for a city. Get into a hostel. He hated that. Preferred to be out on the hills, not in the big towns. Grey buildings, grey people. Some days you never saw the sky. They stole your things, city people, and he had to smuggle the dog in and out. He sniffed the air. Snow on the wind. He would set a good fire tonight with those papers, cook up a bite of food . . . sausages. All he needed now were some sausages.

'Smell any sausages boy?' he spoke to his dog. 'Eh?' He shook the worn leather lead. The dog turned intelligent eyes towards him. 'Come on then. Let's go into the village and round the back of the hotel and have a look there.' Sam pulled gently on the lead, and man and dog shuffled off in the direction of a small straggle of houses further up the road.

Constable McClusky checked the thermometer on the station wall. It was dropping steadily. Winter on the way, he thought. It was going to be a cold one, and he had pulled duty on the roster for the night shift. He looked around the tiny station. Nothing left to see to. All the reports were done. He'd read every bulletin and update from HQ. Tidied up, swept out the cell. Now he was bored. It was going to be a long night.

He walked to the window and looked down the main street. There was old Sam. A 'gentleman of the road' was his dad's phrase. Casualties of care in the community, he called them. Most of the ones he saw had mental problems. Must be hard on them this time of year, bitter wind, snow forecast. He looked back at the empty cell. Why not? It would be some company and he knew the old man could play chess. He put some soup on the stove.

'God bless you, son.' The old man sat down gratefully. He took the bread from the plate, broke off a piece and gave it to the dog. 'Always feed the dog first,' he said. 'Smart dog, that. See what he found me tonight, eh?' He pointed to the carrier bags lying on the floor beside him.

Constable McClusky hardly glanced at them. He went to the cupboard to bring out soup bowls and spoons. His back was to the table as Sam began to take some of the newspapers out.

'Recycling,' said Sam. 'Recycling. They think they've just invented it. Been doing it for donkeys. Take newspapers for instance. You can burn 'em, wear 'em and read 'em. Not in that order, of course.' He opened one out and looked it up and down. 'Oh,' he said. He reached for another, and then another. 'Now, that's not very nice,' he said.

'What's the matter?' asked Constable McClusky, putting the dishes down on the table and crossing to the stove.

'Somebody gone and cut bits out of them all,' said Sam. 'See?' He held one up as the policeman turned round to look.

'Ach well, never mind. I'll shove them in the stove.'

The old man muttered away as he ate his soup. 'Imagine cutting bits out the paper. Weren't even the picture bits. Just the print. I mean who would want to do that?'

'Who indeed?' McClusky nodded and smiled. He hoped the old guy wasn't going to rabbit on about his newspapers all night. 'Fancy a game of chess?' he said, and took the board and box out from the bottom drawer of the filing cabinet.

'Sure son, sure,' said Sam. He patted the dog and stretched out his feet towards the stove.

McClusky set out the pieces and moved the pile of newspapers to one side. He glanced at them. Sections cut out, and quite neatly, too, with scissors. Some strict religious folks lived around here. Probably they would be censoring the salacious pictures. But Sam had said it wasn't

126

the photographs which had gone. The old man's words echoed in his head. Who would want to cut words out of newspapers? Never mind, thought McClusky. Let's decide an opening gambit. He knew Sam could play a good game. Shlinovsky's defence? Pawn to rook four.

Constable McClusky's hand had just closed round the white pawn when a recollection of one of tonight's official bulletins came into his head. *Be on the lookout for . . .*

He placed the chess piece back on the board and got up slowly.

'Ready, son?' asked Sam.

'Uh . . . just a minute,' said McClusky. He looked on his desk. There it was. He re-read it slowly. *Bombing attacks. Area – Scottish Borders. Anonymous tip-off . . . Letters cut from newspapers.* It couldn't be . . . He hesitated. He could be made to look helluva stupid at HQ if the rest of boys heard. He imagined the staff magazine: 'McClusky collars old Sam and his wee dog' with a suitable Hamish MacBeth-type cartoon to accompany it of course.

He swung round in his chair. The old man was dozing by the fire.

'Sam,' he said. 'Those newspapers, where did you get them?'

McClusky listened to Sam as he looked through the bundle of papers, examining each one carefully. Then he studied the memo from HQ again and saw the direct information line number typed large along the bottom.

He sat back down at his desk and picked up the telephone.

16 Incident three – Longheath?

Maxwell was weary. They were running out of time. He was slumped right down in his chair when his deputy came into the room.

'We might have something.' John spoke as soon as he opened the door. 'A whisper on the wind . . . nothing more.'

Maxwell sat up at once.

'CAL,' said the deputy. 'Only one word. It came via an informant who was in jail in South America six months ago with a drug-dealer. Among all the other stuff this name was mentioned. The grass didn't pay any attention. He'd been put in to ferret info on the drug supply. The only thing that stuck in his head was something about bombs. CAL loved explosions . . .' The deputy grimaced. 'That's all.'

'CAL,' said Maxwell. 'Is that his code name?'

His deputy shook his head. 'Nobody knows. They went back down the source line and there's no additional details. In fact, it came in with masses of different information, but was sifted out by one sharp-eyed female intelligence officer.'

Maxwell raised an eyebrow.

'C.A.L.' said his deputy. 'Crosston . . . Altminster . . . Perhaps L next?'

'Good work,' said Maxwell. He sighed. 'Or a coincidence . . . ?'

His deputy made a face. 'Don't think so. It's quite a neat fit. He's probably travelling under a different ID, but they're beginning to look through the transatlantic passenger lists.'

'And we'll get the name of every town in Britain beginning with the letter L,' said Maxwell.

'Done it,' said the deputy. He put a computer printout on the table.

'There's a lot,' said Maxwell.

'Not so many as we won't catch him.'

'Before or after?'

Just as his deputy opened his mouth to reply the red telephone on the table rang.

'There's a Constable McClusky on the line,' said the intelligence operator. 'He's a bit nervous about it all, but I think he might have something for you.'

'A village called Teal,' said Maxwell, an hour or so later, 'just south of Edinburgh.' Maxwell highlighted a tiny dot among the Lammermuir Hills. 'Both previous targets were within striking distance of it.' He smiled grimly. 'We're closing in.' Then he raised his hand quickly. 'I know, John, I know. If he's aiming to be active on Saturday then he's probably long gone by now. But run a softly-softly investigation on all hotels, boarding houses, B&Bs . . .' He heaved a sigh. 'There will be dozens of them in that type of area, up every farm lane, down every road end. Observe and report back. Nobody moves in. He's dangerous . . . and, also, I want him caught, not scared off and left out there to begin again. Let them know how important it is, tell them to do their best . . . unobtrusively.'

'The locals will laugh if we try to do anything unobtrusive up there,' said the deputy. 'But don't worry.' He grinned. 'I'm a country boy myself. All that's needed is to brief the mobile librarian, the village post office and the travelling shop. The whole area will be alerted by teatime.'

'What about the old man who found the newspapers?' asked Maxwell.

His deputy shook his head. 'He's well known in the area. All up and down the east coast in fact. Spends most of the year travelling, then heads for Edinburgh or

Newcastle as the winter comes on. He's clean. He wouldn't be able to hold the scissors steady enough anyway, far less have an envelope and a stamp. Under the rules for institutional care he's assessed as 'being able to cope'. The only damage he's likely to do is to himself. The constable reckons one of these cold spells they'll find him frozen to death. That's why he brought him in last night. Against regulations, of course, but . . . lucky for us. The lab says the warning message was definitely cut from those papers.'

Maxwell studied the map again. 'Not only is Teal within a day's drive from the two hits, it is also –' he picked up a ruler, '– as the crow flies, almost equidistant. See?' And now it was his turn to be excited. 'Look, John!' he said, measuring the space on the map. 'They are practically the same distance away from the centrepoint.' He dropped the ruler suddenly and, crossing the room quickly, began searching in the drawers of the desk. 'Now let's see what this gives us!' he cried holding up a pair of compasses. He screwed his pencil in firmly and, placing the point directly on top of Teal, he swung the compass in an arc, making a wide circle on the map. The pencil mark went several kilometres beyond Crosston and fell short of Altminster by about thirty.

He looked at his deputy. 'What do you reckon?'

'Close enough to follow it up,' said the deputy. He

picked up a magnifying glass and tracked the circumference of the circle centimetre by centimetre on the map. 'There are three towns whose names begin with the letter L situated reasonably close to our catchment line.' He scribbled them down quickly and handed the paper to Maxwell. Maxwell read them out slowly.

'Littlemill . . . Lochendrick . . . and . . . Longheath.'

17 Rendez-vous ice rink

Sarah, Phil, David and Maggie were making plans for the weekend.

'Are we skating tomorrow?' asked David as they left the school that Friday night.

'Could there possibly be another six girls that you have arranged to meet at the ice rink by any chance?' Sarah asked him. 'Or are you becoming a fitness freak?'

'No,' said David. 'Kirsty and I are going out for a meal tomorrow night. I meant the four of us tomorrow morning. We'll have to keep up our health and strength if we intend going on the selection weekend.'

'I'm not sure if I *will* go,' said Maggie.

'Oh,' said Sarah. She turned to her friend. 'Why not? It won't be the same without you.'

'Well, I don't think I would enjoy it all that much, Sarah. All that drilling and training, and camping out at night in the cold and dark.' She shivered. 'Having to go to the toilet in a field.' She wrinkled up her nose. 'Communal showers . . .'

'Won't you give it a try at least?' begged Sarah.

Maggie shook her head. 'There's no point. Truthfully I don't think it's for me.'

'Nor for me,' said Phil. He looked at Sarah and then looked away. 'But I'll come skating tomorrow with you.'

'Oh,' said Sarah again. She felt terribly let down.

David leaned up against her arm. 'I'm still game. We will have a great time together, Sarah, babe. Never mind those two stay-at-homes. We'll yomp every morning at sun-up, and chomp every evening at sun-down.'

Phil pushed David away from Sarah. 'Chill out. You don't mind too much do you?' he asked Sarah anxiously.

'Well, I do, actually,' said Sarah plaintively. 'I thought it would be fun to go away in a group together.'

'They don't realise what they'll be missing,' said David. 'We'll have beer in the bar at bath-time, and midnight feasts at . . . at . . . well, midnight probably.'

'Go away, Dave.' Phil aimed a punch at his friend.

'We'll have sing-songs on the bus on the journey home,' David went on, dancing around just out of Phil's reach. 'And when we get back we won't tell you *any* of our secrets. So there! Naa-naa-na-naa-naa!'

Phil broke away from the group to chase David along the road. He caught up with him easily and, grabbing him by the ear, dragged him back to where the girls were standing.

'Just wait until I'm a super-fit member of the Commando Corps,' said David, when Phil eventually let him go. He rubbed his ear. 'I'll come back and stomp all over you.'

'It's very likely that they'll split friends up anyway,' said Maggie. 'There are would-be cadets coming from all over the country. You and David probably won't even see each other.'

'Probably,' Sarah agreed slowly. She supposed it was silly to have thought it would turn out like some great game. From the description Ben had given them, the weekend was obviously designed to contain training and tests under intensive conditions. But, nevertheless, she was disappointed that her other two friends weren't going along. Or . . . was she more upset because Phil wasn't? And not just because she would miss his company, which she did enjoy so much . . . There was a deeper seam here to follow. Now she could not ignore the fact that they were not the same. And it was an aspect which concerned her.

True, they had lots in common, a shared sense of humour and love of sport. But she suspected Phil's reason was not that he would mind the discomfort so much, or that he wouldn't be able to keep up with the rest – he was the fittest of them all – Sarah feared it was because he had decided that he didn't want to be associated with something that she was beginning to enjoy more and more and found challenging and exciting.

Phil took her hand as they walked along the road. 'Don't look at me like that, Sarah Bell. I haven't said I definitely *won't* go.'

When they got to the traffic-lights Sarah looked at her watch. 'I'd better move,' she said. 'I've to meet my mum at the health centre.'

'I'll see you tomorrow morning at the Pyramid Centre,' said Phil. He touched Sarah on the shoulder as she moved away.

Sarah smiled at him. 'Don't be too late then. I'm going shopping in the afternoon.'

Phil grimaced and Maggie laughed. 'Not for boots, I hope,' he called after her.

'The Pyramid Centre, Longheath,' Maxwell said the name aloud and using his laser pointer he spotlighted the town on the map. 'Lochendrick, possible focus there, the sports complex, and Littlemill . . . harder to suggest a likely target here. There's a small shopping mall or bus station which may attract our friend's attentions.'

He clicked his pointer on to the two other towns and then switched it off. 'You all know why we have chosen to cover those three particular towns this weekend. The reason I've picked out these specific locations is because they are within a very nebulous pattern which this bomber is following. They are soft targets, areas which are crowded with people going about their business. The previous bombings have been where civilians have been gathered.'

Maxwell walked to the front of the room to face his team. 'We have enough information to believe that we are tracking an armed and extremely dangerous person. He has killed before and will do so again. He is extremely clever and cool under pressure.' Maxwell looked at them steadily. 'But the above applies to all of you.'

He indicated three piles of folders. 'We are dividing into three groups, each with a section commander, to cover each location. I myself will lead one team. Each person will take a file relating to the area he's covering. The location listings are on the board.'

Maxwell picked up a folder from the bundle marked Longheath and handed it to the man sitting in the front row. 'I'd like you to be one of the team at Longheath,

Gavin,' he said. 'And I want you covering the skating rink: There are detailed plans there showing exits, entrances, sizes, everything. Read it through, then I'll brief you, then study it again. I want you to be as familiar with that area as if it was your own backyard. Your life – a lot of lives – may depend on it.'

Gavin McMurtchie had started his training years ago in Northern Ireland. The city footpatrols in the streets of Belfast and Londonderry were the most hazardous in the world. On tail-end Charlie duty with his squad, last in the line moving backwards down the alleyways, eyes on every rooftop, doorway and window, he had survived when many of his comrades had been cut down. Later he was among the first detachment of paras to be dropped on the Falkland Islands. He had operated behind enemy lines in the Arabian desert and in the bandit country of South Armagh. Now he opened up the file his commanding officer had given him and began to study the papers inside.

Two hours later, when everyone had left for food and some rest, Maxwell read through his own notes again thoroughly. Then he sat for a long time going over his strategies. There would be one final briefing, and then by the early hours of the morning his personnel would be in place. He should get some rest himself, he thought. He switched off the projector and glanced at the main map again. His eyes kept coming back to Longheath. He crossed to the big operations table running along one side of the room and studied the aerial reconnaissance pictures. Then, walking slowly down the length of the room, he looked at the photographs of the shopping mall, all the trade outlets, the cafés and bars. He sat down at the computer screen and brought up the three town centres, one by one.

Logically it should be Lochendrick. Littlemill was too small. A stranger would be easily spotted in the town which really wasn't much more than a large village. Also, an explosion there wouldn't cause enough aggro to satisfy this particular bomber. Not sufficient people to maim and murder. Not enough attention, not a big enough splash in the papers. And Longheath was a bad site for a getaway. Congested roads in the town centre meant that you could be caught in your own explosion. It was also perhaps not big enough to create the havoc this bomber obviously wanted to see.

Yes, it should be Lochendrick. The biggest town . . . huge sports complex with shops alongside. It was wide open. A plump picking for a hungry wolf.

Yet . . .

He keyed in the code reference and the Pyramid Centre showed on the screen again. He clicked the mouse on the ice rink. Looking at it . . . thinking in the same way, unknown to him, as Sarah Bell had done weeks earlier.

He spoke his thought aloud.

'That is an ideal terrorist's target.'

And . . . he reflected, he had chosen Gavin to be there. Why? An unconscious instinctive decision which meant that his best agent would be in the most vulnerable spot in the complex.

Also . . . something else . . . He rubbed the deep line which ran from the bridge of his nose to his hairline. The undefinable . . . the awareness that had saved his life on at least two previous occasions. That sixth sense that made him recognise the booby-trapped school bus, the too-easily-available safety spot in which to shelter, which proved to be the place where the land mines lay. The empty doorway tempting him to take shelter there, but covered by a sniper on the rooftop opposite. That unknown instinct . . .

By the time of the final meeting, late on Friday night, they had one more piece of information. A postmistress in a village fifteen or so kilometres from Teal thought she might have seen a strange car . . . and she was almost sure the driver was wearing a purple jacket. She only caught a glimpse, but had remembered, because it had the same pattern as her son's: a green zigzag sleeve detail.

Maxwell spoke to his men and wished them luck. He

knew that the medical teams had been put on secret standby at Lochendrick. Despite this, and the fact that police attention was to be focused there, Maxwell made his decision. He informed the two other section commanders. 'Tomorrow . . . I think I'll take charge at Longheath.'

18 Sniper's nest

Sarah's mother was preoccupied and tense when Sarah met her at the health centre.

'Lochendrick Health Centre were in touch today. There's a Black Alert on up there,' she said.

'What's that?' asked Sarah.

'It means they have no definite confirmation, but potential criminal or subversive activities are suspected.'

'Your friend works there, doesn't she?' said Sarah. 'Do you think she's in some kind of danger?'

'I don't know. She thinks it's all a flap about nothing. They were told not to be too alarmed, but were "requested to be vigilant". She thought that the idea of any office worker being vigilant late on a Friday afternoon was hysterically funny.'

'Well it does sound like a contradiction in terms,' agreed Sarah.

'Yes . . . but then she phoned me back a few minutes ago to say that the police had asked her to come in tomorrow morning. They want her to log on the computers and keep the phone lines open.'

Sarah raised her eyebrows. 'So . . . ?'

Her mother slipped on her coat and gathered up her briefcase. 'Well it sounds a little more serious now, doesn't it?'

Later that evening, as they settled down to eat supper, Sarah's mum told her dad about the Black Alert at Lochendrick.

'It's a bit worrying, don't you think?' she said. 'We wondered if the police were planning some special operation there tomorrow.'

Her dad winked at Sarah as he handed round some napkins. 'That's an old civil service dodge,' he said. 'Everybody knows about it. They use it in public buildings at Hogmanay, or just before a long weekend. The staff "acting on information received" declare a "Black Alert". All rooms must be cleared and examined. It means they are allowed to ask visitors to leave early, before official closing time. Then all the staff skive off home.'

Sarah laughed. 'Is that true?'

'Yes,' said her dad, '. . . and no.'

Sarah's mum put down her fork. 'What do you mean? You know something, don't you?'

'I know that there are medical teams on secret standby in the Lochendrick area tomorrow.' He looked at his wife, Sarah and then Gran. '*Secret* standby,' he repeated. 'I don't have to emphasise that do I?' He looked at his wife. 'I was going to tell you later anyway, only I thought we might enjoy our supper first. I'm going up there with my crew early in the morning.'

'You could be in danger,' said Sarah.

Her dad shook his head. 'Not where I've been stationed. The story is we're doing a simulated disaster exercise in one of the rugby pitches on the outskirts of the town. But there's a strong rumour that a huge undercover operation is taking place in the centre. We're probably there as a precaution.' He shrugged. 'Whether they actually know anything or not is anybody's guess.'

Sarah's gran shook her head. 'These intelligence chappies are quite clever though, aren't they? I'll bet they've got wind of a bank robbery or something.' She gave Sarah's arm a squeeze. 'Is our trip out tomorrow still on?'

'Of course,' said Sarah. 'I'm skating with my friends in the morning, and then you and I will hit the shops in the afternoon. I want to show you this dress I'm going to buy for the school's Christmas disco.'

'And, are you going to the disco with that nice young man I've heard you talking about so often? What's his name? Philip?'

Sarah blushed. 'I didn't realise that I was talking about him so often,' she said. 'I suppose I might see him there. I *do* have other male friends you know.'

'I'm sure you do,' said her gran, and she squeezed Sarah's arm again. 'Although isn't he a bit special?'

'Yes, but . . .' Sarah paused. She was aware that her mum and dad were now paying close attention. 'Oh, I don't know. He says he might not go on the Army selection weekend.'

'Is everyone else going?' asked her mum.

'No, Maggie's decided she's not.'

'Well then,' said her mum.

'But we all knew that Maggie would drop out eventually,' said Sarah. 'She never really liked it much. She only went along in the first place to keep me company.'

'Wasn't that Phil's reason for going too?' asked her dad.

Sarah thought for a moment. 'Not entirely.' Though she supposed it was partly true. She had been keen to find out about the Army and had persuaded the others to come along as well. 'I thought he'd like it as much as I do. And now I see he doesn't . . .'

Her mum leaned over and took her hand. 'Do you think that this creates a gulf between the two of you? Is it upsetting you?'

'I think it's showing up a basic difference, yes,' said Sarah slowly. 'Whether it is, or will be in the future, a huge gulf . . . I just don't know . . .' she tailed off sadly.

'And obviously, you like him a lot,' said her dad.

Sarah nodded.

'Well that's the main thing,' said Gran. She waved her fork at Sarah. '*Liking* someone is *very* important indeed. There were a great deal of differences between your grandfather and me, but differences can make life more interesting.' She looked at Sarah carefully and then asked her, 'Did Phil tell you that you shouldn't take part in the selection weekend? Did he try to persuade you not to go?'

'No.'

'Well that's a good sign. It means he's not trying to mould you into his way of thinking. Now . . .' her gran paused, 'the hard bit is for you to accept him as *he* is.' She looked at Sarah's face again. 'However, this is Friday night and we shouldn't be having such serious conversations. Tell me about this dress . . .'

Among the girders that made up the roof of the Pyramid Centre a man was moving quietly. Gavin McMurtchie crawled along the electrician's access tunnel and then, reaching a crossbeam, he swung himself down and dropped lightly on to the metal framework which housed the PA system. Ignoring the void below, he jumped across the gap. Then he crouched low and taking out his night-sight binoculars he studied the area he had been assigned to cover.

In the half-dark the ice glowed beneath him, translucent, shimmering. He turned his head slowly, picking out the surroundings carefully. As he surveyed his terrain, sweeping in a long semicircle with the glasses, he began to relax. He had been moving among the steel struts for the best part of an hour as he searched for the place which would give him his best field of vision.

'The rink,' Maxwell had instructed him, 'Is the most vulnerable point. I want it sussed. The ice, the benches, spectators' gallery, the lot. Find an operating locus where you can't be blocked. See, but don't be seen.'

Gavin settled back on his heels. His mouth turned up at the corner and he nodded his head. He had found his spot.

He looked around him, making notes in his head of what he would need to bring up here. Then he looked through the binoculars again and began to memorise the positions of the most distinct features far below him, estimating the range from his own position and the distances between. He returned to operational HQ and reported everything to Maxwell and together they drew up a map, agreeing on grid references and code names. Then Gavin went to bed for a few hours.

By dawn he was up, had eaten breakfast, and was back building his sniper's nest. The camouflage was vital. Black track suit, no buckles and brasses – he had even taken off his wedding ring. Any single thing that could act as a mirror put him in peril. The roof was his chief worry. A thousand pieces of glass arced above him. He squinted upwards trying to assess how bright it would be at the different points of the sun's course in the sky. The weather forecast was fine drizzle, occasional clear spells. He moved further in and looked again. He was now in the shadow, but would have to remember to stay back. He checked and rechecked his own clothes. Everything dark, face blacked, rifle cammed-up, and wearing nothing to reflect either down or across which might create the giveaway glint that would alert the pursued.

Next, he scanned his observation points, aware that distances alter in different light. He adjusted his range findings fraction by fraction until he was satisfied.

Finally, he held the rifle against his cheek and moved it slowly around, assessing his field of fire.

Preparation complete, he called in on the radio and cross-checked the grid references in meticulous detail.

By first light on the Saturday morning he was settled in his place. Tucked up snugly with his back against the crook of the metal struts, Gavin cradled his rifle across his knees, and settled down to wait.

19 Grid-point interlock

At exactly nine forty-seven on Saturday morning Cal entered the Pyramid Centre by the west door. It was the one which led directly in from the bus station.

Best way really . . . even though it meant walking the last kilometre or so from where the car had been left. Basic rule of urban warfare – always cover your trail. Like coming off the hill after a climb. Go down . . . track to the left . . . down . . . switch back to the right . . . down . . . walk across . . . down . . . back again.

Cal found the large colour-coded orientation plan and studied it for a moment or two. It was warm inside, just as well the heavy jacket was in the holdall . . . more comfortable . . . and it meant those three little packages were carefully covered up . . . maybe should keep the cap on meantime though. Cal smiled. A master of disguise.

Ten minutes later Sarah and her friends met up inside the Pyramid Centre. 'Anyone for the shops this afternoon?' Maggie asked as they headed towards the ice rink.

'There is no way I'm going shopping with you again. Ever,' said David. 'You waste so much time trailing round dozens of places. For no reason at all.'

'But we have to,' protested Sarah. 'Otherwise we might not see the very thing we want.'

Maggie placed a hand on Sarah's arm. '*Need*,' she corrected her. 'Not *want*, dear, *need*. Shopping is a *need*.'

'You seem to miss the point,' said Phil. 'The reason for going to a shop is to buy a specific item. One goes shopping to buy something that one wants. That's the reason for going.' He looked at the two girls. 'Isn't it?'

Maggie shook her head. 'No,' she said patiently. 'One goes to the shops to *find out* what one wants to buy. How do you know what you want to buy until you've actually seen it?'

Phil threw his hands in the air. 'I give up.'

'Well, you won't be troubled this afternoon anyway,' said Sarah. 'My gran is meeting me here later. She likes to do her Christmas shopping early and I said I'd go along with her. I help her choose the presents for my wee cousins. She gets terribly confused between Power Rangers, remote-control motors and She-man models.'

'You mean *He*-man,' said David.

'I know what I mean,' said Sarah.

'Are you intending to buy a model car?' said Phil, with sudden interest. 'If it's remote controls you want then they've got some terrific sports-car models in Hackney's store. I could come along with you and help you choose.'

'Aha!' said Maggie. 'Now you've changed your tune! When it's space toys, motors or computer games, then blokes think it's all right to take hours to choose.'

'That's a completely different situation,' said David.

'Why?'

'There are important technical details to consider. It's a serious business. You have to be sure that you select exactly the right kind of vehicle. I mean, there are dozens of specifications which you wouldn't even begin to understand.'

As Phil and Sarah walked ahead they could still hear Maggie and David arguing cheerfully. They were soon separated in the surging crowd of people.

'Ouch!' said Sarah, as someone pushed against her. 'It *is* busy today.'

'Yeah,' said Phil. 'Start of Christmas-shopping-mania.'

They reached the ice rink well ahead of the other two.

'Will we wait for them?' Sarah asked.

'Nah,' said Phil. 'Let's get on the ice. They'll catch up.'

At the edge of the ice Cal paused, touched the holdall, pale eyes glittering. More precious than the crown jewels, this one. Three neat parcels to be posted . . . Where?

In the queue at the ticket desk Sarah and Phil were split up. Phil eventually picked up his skating-boots and turned away from the counter. He paused for a moment, searching to see where Sarah had gone. She was on the ice already. He smiled as he watched her, copper hair flying out.

Cal sat down on the top row of the spectators' gallery, put the holdall on the ground, took out one plastic carrier bag and slid it under the seat in front and, looking down at the ice, saw the girl with the reddish-gold hair.

And Gavin McMurtchie saw Cal. Flickered for a second in his sight-finder . . . and moved on.

Cal picked up the holdall. Strange . . . for such a deadly bundle it didn't weigh much. Better move now. No use wasting time. But . . . the skaters were good to watch, relaxing . . . yet powerful. Effortlessly gliding along . . . then a sudden surge of energy. Hidden energy, ready to burst forth . . . A bit like this. Unconsciously Cal patted the holdall.

And the movement, caught in the tail end of Gavin McMurtchie's sweep, registered. He stopped, brought the binoculars back, and focused. Then he reached for his radio.

'A possible on the gallery.'

In the security office with the closed-circuit television screens, where Maxwell had established his centre of operations, the radio crackled. Maxwell bent his head, and then swung his eyes to the video screens. The spectators' gallery showed a wide-angle view from far back. It was now empty.

Gavin counted seconds in his head, estimated the man's walk and the time it would take him to come down the stairs, trying to second guess which exit on to the shopping mall he would use.

Cal sauntered out towards the row of benches. Leaned over the perimeter rail and dropped another bag down into the gap between the back of the seat and the wall.

Maxwell's radio crackled again. His eyes concentrated hard on the television screens. Then he leaned forward and spoke into his own transmitter.

Phil looked back to see if Maggie and David were following and . . . frowned. Suddenly there was a large man at the ticket desk speaking to the assistant. He turned to the queue that had built up behind him and spoke to them, joking and laughing. Then he turned back and, reaching up, he pulled the steel shutter down, closing the hatch off.

Tough on them, thought Phil. The ice must be too busy. Well at least he and Sarah could have some fun for a while.

A line appeared across Maxwell's forehead as he watched Cal hesitate and then begin to walk between the benches. Saw the figure stop and sit down in the very front row.

'A. B. C.' said Cal softly. 'One . . . Two . . .'

Placed the third package under the bench . . . 'Three.'

Now, really should put on the heavy jacket for going out again. Don't want to catch cold. Took it from the holdall and standing up, slipped it on. A particular type of jacket: purple, with green zigzag sleeve detail.

* * *

Maxwell's radio leaped to life. 'I see it,' he said. 'I see it.' He picked up the microphone which connected directly with Gavin McMurtchie's earphones and spoke clearly and distinctly.

And high in the meshed steel overhang that held the lighting fixtures Gavin McMurtchle received the message. He set down his binoculars and lifted his rifle.

Phil finished lacing his boots and stepped on to the ice. Now where was she? He searched the rink again and then spotted Sarah on her own almost at the far side. The tall figure with the long copper curls was easy to find; she stood out in a crowd. Except . . . Phil thought for a second . . . there was no crowd. In fact, it was very quiet in the rink for a Saturday morning. He looked back again at the ticket desk. It was still firmly closed, and he couldn't see his friends now. Phil frowned again. What was going on?

Maxwell's eyes flicked back to the main monitor. Better be extra cautious with this one. It would soon become obvious that the rink was being cleared. 'Make the announcement,' he told the manager of the Pyramid Centre. Almost at once the loudspeakers boomed, informing the public that a curling practice was scheduled in fifteen minutes time.

Maxwell was deeply uneasy. It was too neat. Within minutes his men would have closed in, yet, he was worried. He checked his screens. Was there any member of the public close enough to this lunatic to be in danger? There were another two figures further along the benches, a woman with a young child. Potential hostages if anything went wrong. What else was in the holdall? No more bombs, of that he was convinced. He had guessed three, and three had been planted. He was sure that was all there were. And he had another reason to think that the mission had been accomplished. There was a purposeful movement to the bomber's walk now. The job was done. Time to leave.

But . . . there could be a weapon in the holdall, or concealed inside the jacket. This guy liked killing, was merciless . . . If he sussed what was happening.

God Almighty – he had stopped.

Why?

Maxwell's eyes flicked to the screens. There was a young couple on the ice . . .

What . . . ? What the hell were they doing?

20 Target will fall when hit

Phil heard the announcement about the curling practice and immediately relaxed. It was all this Army training, he thought. It had set him on edge, trying to be ever alert to deal with danger. He smiled at himself, and was still smiling as he caught up with Sarah.

'What are you looking so pleased about?' she asked.

'Because I've got you all to myself,' he said. 'They've closed the hatch. There's a curling practice due to begin, and David and Maggie didn't get on the ice.' He took her arm. 'Come on. Let's skate. We won't have much time. They'll probably chase us off soon.'

Gavin watched the scene below. Stretched out on his stomach, left hand forward, wrist straight and locked, his rifle lying across the open palm.

'OK,' said Sarah. 'Let's go right across.' She pointed to where Cal was standing.

What the hell is the girl doing? thought Maxwell. And then he realised what Sarah was pointing to. The barrier break. One of the openings on to the ice. About five metres from where Cal was standing.

'Jeez,' he whispered.

Cal stopped. It was wonderful. Ice-skating. Memories came back. In the park with Mamma. A happy, happy childhood. Sliding on the hard glassy surface, falling with a bump, and laughing at Mamma's face. And then in Switzerland, the chill of the frosty air in your lungs, the hiss of the blades. Cries of birds across the lake as they rose into the air in a great clumsy panic. Faster, faster . . . Cal blinked. But it had been ruined. All of it. Things got confused. It wasn't possible to go back home they said, and Mamma had agreed with them. Placed in a sanatorium . . . 'For your own sake, dear.' Cal's face twisted with hatred. A safe place, a nowhere place. Out of sight of the world, away from the public gaze. Where no one knew . . . Well after today, everyone would know.

* * *

Gavin's earphones were clamped firmly to his head. He heard Maxwell's every word as he thought aloud.

'Why has he stopped?' said Maxwell. 'What is he looking at? What is he up to?'

Gavin shifted slightly so that his left elbow was directly below the rifle barrel.

The target had walked a few more metres closer to the child and its mother. Hesitated, stopped, looked around ... and now ... up ... Gavin knew he couldn't be seen. He had built OPs in Bosnia, and made hides on Fenwick Moor among the barren and inhospitable bracken. He watched the lone figure far below him. He was confident of his camouflage. But ... it always made your heart stand for a second when a target stared right at you like that ...

And ... McMurtchie's eyes narrowed. Something else ...?

Maxwell, too, had had a bad moment when the target had turned and stared at him. Directly into the camera. Had someone been careless? A glint of metal from the rifle barrel? Some slight movement? No, he had confidence in Gavin's skills in surveillance and camouflage.

But why then had the bomber stopped? He should be leaving, smartish.

Maxwell glanced back at the main monitor. His personnel, dressed in the Pyramid Centre's track suits, were keeping people off the ice, ostensibly because of the curling. But would a trained terrorist not recognise the difference in their manner from that of an ordinary rink attendant?

He *must* be suspicious. It was too obvious the way the rink was emptying. The absence of spectators on the surrounding seats. He surely could see that the mall was quieter, that there were no queues at the food outlets.

Sarah looked around as she took Phil's hand. 'They seem to have cleared a lot of people off. There's hardly anybody here, just that woman with her little kid and that young guy with the cap on over there . . .'

Phil's heart gave an unexpected lurch as she spoke. And then he laughed at himself. Hyped-up by Ben with his assault courses and command tasks, he was assessing every situation as a possible Army exercise. Stupid. Yet . . . he thought of the man at the ticket desk who, only a few moments ago, had so abruptly pulled the steel grid down. Those flinty eyes. Similar, in fact, to the recruiting officer who had come to the school. The set of his shoulders . . . God, he was becoming neurotic.

'Well if we have to get off, let's make it the long way,' said Sarah. 'Let's skate right across the ice and then go off at the barrier break.'

Gavin put his right hand on his rifle stock, thumb over the top and laid it against his cheek. His finger was on the trigger, just touching.

Cal stopped again and looked around, and then up at the roof where the glass made a wondrous mosaic, reflecting colour all around. Beautiful . . .

Gavin zeroed in on the target, cross hairs over the chest. Disabling body shot.

Maxwell estimated the connection time with the mother and child in seconds. The couple on the ice were beginning to skate, to pick up speed, heading straight for where Cal stood . . .

. . . and suddenly the figure of the bomber raised its hand.

Cal knew it was dangerous to wait, but ice was magnetic, drawing attention, and it was fun to watch the boy and the girl with the copper-coloured hair . . .

* * *

And thinking about hair, Cal's hand reached up to take off the cap.

Maxwell's voice spoke in Gavin's ear.

And Gavin didn't hesitate. As the cap came off, and his unspoken 'something different' query was answered, and the long blonde hair tumbled free, and he realised the face raised to his was that of a girl . . . he didn't falter. His hold didn't slacken, and the trigger slotted right back.

Cal shook her hair out around her shoulders. That felt good. Cool air on her face, through her hair. Much better, she thought.

It was the last thought she ever had.

Gavin McMurtchie's bullet slammed into her upper chest. It glanced off her right shoulder blade and deflected into her throat, going straight up through her face and out at the top of her skull.

Fleetingly in McMurtchie's head was the image of his own teenage daughter. Then briskly he lifted his radio and spoke three words.

'Target taken out.'

21 Dance of death

Sarah heard nothing. Not the crack from the rifle high above her head, nor the small sharp sound which Cal made as the bullet entered her body. But she saw . . . the girl's limbs jerked by a mad puppeteer, arms and legs juddering . . . saw . . . the girl's face exploding . . . saw . . . the girl pitching forwards on to the ice.

Then she herself was brought down in a flying tackle. Thudding on to the ground, Phil came with her and they were propelled further on the slippery surface in the direction of the barrier break. A man's hand pushed her face into the ice. He shouted in her ear and she knew to stay still. She lay there, unable to move, winded, shocked, terrified, but with her eyes still open, staring . . . transfixed by the sight so close to her. The blonde girl . . . and the deep red stain seeping out from under her head.

Phil was more sensitive to the scenes around him as they skated. He was soaking up sound and movement, tracking noise and colour. Noticing the copper glow of Sarah's hair, and how its shade subtly altered as she passed under the different coloured spotlights. Knowing too, somehow, a vague uneasiness. Aware of the loudspeaker announcement as he took Sarah's arm, her laughter, the girl walking round behind the barrier just at the spot they were heading for. Her face looking up to the lights above, her halting at one of the openings on to the ice, reaching up to pull off the grey cap . . . her long hair falling . . . falling . . .

Falling . . . she was falling . . . in a macabre mockery of some ice-dance she tumbled out across the smooth white surface which stretched between them. And she lay there quite still.

Three men appeared on the spectators' benches at the back, running very fast, jumping along and down to reach the rink.

Someone, a man, crashed violently against him and Sarah from behind, throwing them both to the ground.

Screaming, 'DOWN! DOWN!'

And when Phil tried to raise his head to see what was

happening, it was thrust roughly back on to the ice and the order repeated. His eyes remained, then, on a level with the girl's face. Closer, much closer than earlier, because both he and Sarah had slid forward on impact. But the girl's face was shattered . . . the blonde hair flooded with red. Clothes sticky-stained with blood. Blood on her face, on her arms and legs. Blood on the ice.

Neither Sarah nor Phil cried. Not then, or immediately afterwards, although they did later. Both of them.

There was no time. In a clear, carefully controlled sequence of events they were helped gently but firmly from the ice. Their own boots and bags returned to them, someone quickly untied their skates and took them away.

Just in her line of vision Sarah saw the stretcher arrive. The body of the girl was rolled rapidly on to it.

They're not regular paramedics, she thought.

There was no confusion. The whole area was completely cleared, the body removed, the ice washed down, and then began the checking of every centimetre of the rink. The stunning efficiency of the operation was in itself shocking. Phil watched them, half dazed, as he put his own boots back on and clumsily laced them up. It occurred to him that the people moving swiftly about and around him had done this type of work before.

They were taken to a small interview room, and a man who introduced himself as Maxwell told them that their parents had been informed.

'How?' asked Phil in a dazed voice.

'Your addresses were in your wallets in your bags. Don't worry,' Maxwell smiled. 'We've sent a car at once. In case they heard a newsflash.'

And, yes, he knew they had been separated from friends who might be worried about them. They also had been told.

And Phil didn't doubt that they had. Almost impossible to locate Maggie and David in the crush of those ushered out by the side exit, but Phil found he believed this calm smiling man who had brought them both some strong tea, and stood over them coaxing them to drink it.

Maxwell smiled again at their puzzled looks. 'There's a team of people examining this morning's video footage,' he said. 'We spotted you all as you came into the mall. We've managed to ID your friends from that. Someone has spoken to them, and they know that you are safe and well.'

So Sarah and Phil sat holding hands and listened as Maxwell talked quietly, giving them a little information, bit by bit, and sprinkling his conversation occasionally with a question or two. Phil found his casual manner slightly chilling. He chatted about skating and winter sports, about his nephew who played tennis, their schoolwork, how he himself had been useless at exams. 'Absolutely hopeless. My folks thought I'd never get any qualifications, never find a job.'

But when Phil then enquired what he did do for a living, Maxwell paused, then carried on speaking as though the question had never been asked.

Finally, Sarah and Phil's parents arrived. Phil's mum apologised immediately for bringing along his little sister.

'I couldn't say no,' she told everybody. 'She dotes on him and would have gone crazy if we'd left her at home.'

Sarah, watching Phil swing Becky up into his arms and her snuggling close into him, felt her own tears start then. And she could see by the way Phil kept his face turned in towards his sister and held her tightly, that emotion and delayed reactions were beginning to take hold of him. He looked up at Sarah and opened his arms wider. She went to him and huddled close in at his shoulder, and he cuddled his sister and managed to stroke Sarah's hair with his free hand.

It was Maxwell who finally separated them very gently and gave Sarah across to her parents.

In the car travelling home Sarah's dad fretted and fumed so much it almost made her laugh.

'If only I'd known they suspected Longheath might be

targeted I'd never have gone to Lochendrick,' he declared several times.

'You would have had to go to where you were sent,' said Sarah's mum. 'And that *was* where the police and the medics were focused.'

'That chap back there wasn't regular police,' said Sarah's dad. 'He had a look of the Intelligence Service. I'll bet they knew more.'

Her mum shivered. 'Yes,' she said. 'But there's no point in going on about it. If I'd had any inkling at all, then I wouldn't have agreed that Sarah could go skating at the Pyramid Centre this morning, or arrange a shopping trip with Gran this afternoon.' She peered at Sarah's face. 'Let's leave it just now.' She put her arm round Sarah and pulled her closer. 'They advised a doctor see you tonight, and have also offered counselling services. What do you think? They said they would get in touch with the school and see what's best.'

Sarah, her head leaning against her mum's shoulder, only nodded.

It was almost midnight before Maxwell's final debriefing with his deputy. He held up a still from one of the mall's video cameras. A blurred snapshot of the girl's face seconds before her death.

'Christina Alexandra Langley,' he said. 'Otherwise known as Cal.'

'If only we'd had that information earlier,' said his deputy.

'A pity,' agreed Maxwell. 'Identified now as a disaffected member of our aristocracy who cut herself off from her family several years ago at the age of sixteen. Mentally unstable. Spent time in a hospital in Switzerland before discharging herself unofficially. Parents never reported it of course. Family disgrace. She was dangerous, to herself and others. A girl with a grudge. Against authority, her peers, anybody, everybody. Bummed around the world. Joined various underground organisations, but left them almost immediately. They were too tame for her.'

The deputy raised his eyebrows. 'Considering the track record of some of our friends that tells us a lot about the state of her mind.'

Maxwell nodded. 'Decided to go it alone,' he continued. 'Came back to mainland Britain with plenty of materials – guns, ammunition, Semtex, timers etcetera to keep her in business for some time. We think she chose this area to make a statement about because it was where her mother had taken her on holiday when she was very small.'

Maxwell put the picture back on the table. 'Her car has been located, with her personal things, some camping equipment and what we hope is most of the gear.' He shrugged. 'There's no way of telling. If it hadn't been for one smart intelligence officer, a clever village bobby and an observant postmistress we wouldn't have anything. There could be more stuff buried somewhere and we'll never find it. However the clothes in her luggage told us a lot.'

He handed his deputy a sheet of paper.

The deputy glanced down the list of items. 'With so little knowledge about her available it's no wonder we were left chasing air.'

'And naturally,' said Maxwell, 'no one would ever be able to give us a description of someone acting suspiciously because they automatically assumed the bomber was a man. A young girl buying some newspapers in the village shop . . . what's odd about that? In the staff area of the shoe outlet, with her pretty face and long blonde hair, and wearing a black skirt and a white blouse, she would be so unnoticeable as to be almost invisible. At the Remembrance Day service she was in the guise of the most innocent; there was a school uniform among the things in her holdall – shirt, tie, grey pleated skirt . . . Dressed as a schoolgirl she would attract no suspicion whatsoever.'

'We'll get flak for this one,' said his deputy. 'The press will holler "summary execution" – or worse.'

Maxwell spread his hands in front of him in a gesture of resignation. 'There are a lot of people out there who can now go Christmas shopping safely with their children. That's all I care about.' He stood up wearily. 'I'm going home now.' He snapped open the lid of his briefcase and picked up his incident file to put it inside. The grainy photograph of the girl lay on top. He gazed at the image for a moment; the high cheekbones, the sweetheart-shaped face.

'The female of the species,' he murmured. 'More deadly than the male.'

22 More deadly than the male

'She was murdered.' Phil spoke first.

They were sitting outside, almost a week later, at the school rugby pitch waiting the start of an after-school training session. The morning newspapers had carried the story of the official press release pending the investigation into the incident at Longheath Pyramid Centre.

'Murdered,' Phil repeated. He stuffed the paper he had been reading inside his rucksack.

'She was executed,' said David.

Phil raised his eyebrows. 'Whichever.'

Sarah put her hand on his arm. 'The Army were doing their job.'

'Well, they didn't lie anyway,' said Phil bitterly.

'What do you mean?' asked Sarah.

Phil turned to face her. There was an anguished look in his eyes. 'What did Ben say was the unwritten law of the anti-terrorist squads? "Shoot the women first".'

'Hold on,' said David. 'That was a very dangerous, and according to all reports, quite insane lady.'

'I thought that insane people generally receive medical help,' said Phil.

'There was no time to find out what was wrong with her,' said David.

'Well, if you ask me, they didn't wait to find out,' replied Phil.

'Why don't you ask the mother of the child who was killed laying the wreath at the tomb of the Unknown Soldier?' said Maggie shortly.

'Yeah, ask the families and friends of the two OAPs as well,' said David.

Sarah said nothing. She was watching Phil's face.

'If you allow that type of unlawful killing then you're just as bad as they are,' said Phil. 'Worse in fact.'

'It wasn't unlawful killing,' said David.

'The authorities were operating outside the law,' said Phil. 'Let that happen, then look where it leads you – to the Blackshirts. Next step is Nazism.'

'What she was doing was a crime against humanity,' said Maggie.

'This was a special situation. They believed she was armed and dangerous, and on the point of some kind of action. That's why they brought her down.'

'They'd have shot her anyway,' said Phil. He looked at them all one by one. His face was blotched and his mouth trembled as he spoke. 'You know that.'

'So what?' said David suddenly. 'She deserved it.'

Sarah gasped in shock. This to come from David. The joker, the carefree smiling one of their group. She stared at him.

David's eyes locked with Phil's. 'It was a just cause,' he stated firmly, 'and given the circumstances she had to be taken out.'

'You do realise that you are now using *their* jargon,' said Phil sarcastically. 'You are falling for the propaganda, starting to speak like them.'

'Perhaps I don't look on it like that,' replied David. 'Maybe I don't see it as being a case of "them" and "us". It could be that that's the way I want to talk.'

'It's an abuse of the English language,' said Phil desperately. 'They use wordspeak all the time. Can't you see it? Can't you hear it? To "take out", do you know what that is? It used to mean you'd pulled.' He suddenly rounded on David. 'You should recognise that one, Dave.' You of all people. You know what that means. It's getting off with a girl. Well, I've got news for you. It appears as though it doesn't translate that way any more. Now it means "to kill".

'And "blow away"; Phil continued, his voice rising higher and higher. 'You all remember "blow away", don't you? It was what you did with the dandelion clocks. At the end of summer you blew hard on the puffballs to find out what o'clock it was – and – and –' Phil was almost stuttering now. Sarah moved forward to touch him, but he brushed her away. '– and all the seeds scattered; he went on, 'and that was the way you told the time.' Phil puffed out his cheeks and blew into the air. 'It was good fun, wasn't it?' He stopped, and then went on more quietly. 'Except now it doesn't relate to fluffy downy seeds scattering through the air. Now it's someone's brains exploding on the ground.'

Phil stopped talking suddenly.

'Look; said Maggie quickly, 'everyone's a bit fraught, and . . . and traumatised. Maybe we should discuss this later.'

'No; said David, whose face had gone quite white. 'Let's finish this now. These terms are jargon, OK, I agree. But perhaps they are used to cushion soldiers a bit against the reality of a job they have to do.'

Phil flung his hands in the air. 'That's what I'm trying to say; he cried. 'Everybody is avoiding the real meaning.' He waited a second and then spoke very deliberately.

'We're talking death here. Don't you understand? Those words? They mean *killing*. Ending life.' He spoke more loudly. 'It's a verb . . .

'TO KILL,' he shouted.

'I KILL.

'YOU KILL.

'HE, SHE, OR IT, KILLS.'

'Exactly,' David shouted back. '*She* killed . . . and that's part of the problem, isn't it? Because it was a female. Her photograph is appearing on news stands all over the world, and everybody sees this pretty face . . .'

'There wasn't much left of her face when I saw it,' Phil interrupted. 'Sarah and I were there, remember, on the ice.'

David ignored him and went on. 'There's a picture of a beautiful girl on the TV bulletins. She's smiling out from the front page of the newspapers. Long blonde hair, blue eyes . . . *that's* propaganda and media manipulation. What they should have done is put the murdered kid's class photograph right beside her.' He glared at Phil. 'They're absolutely right when they say shoot the women first.'

'You've been indoctrinated,' said Phil.

'And you're not in the real world, mate,' said David. 'You're sitting in an ivory tower reading poems that don't bear any relation to what is going on outside.'

'That's completely untrue,' said Phil. 'The War Poets

were in fact telling people *exactly* what was going on. But nobody was listening.'

'Oh, forget it,' said David wearily. 'You've made up your mind, and that's it. You don't receive alternatives. You've closed down the communication channels. You're so sure about it all. It's black or white, right or wrong. There is no point in discussing it with you.' David got up, snatched his rucksack, and walked quickly towards the sports pavilion.

Maggie looked wretchedly at Phil, and then at David's retreating back. She flapped her hand in an agitated manner. 'I'll go after him,' she said. 'For goodness sake, calm down Phil. We're all stressed out. Maybe this isn't the right time for you to make noble declarations.' She jumped up and ran off to catch up with David.

Phil turned to Sarah. 'They broke the rules. Although . . . I can't reconcile myself to the fact that there are rules for war, anyway,' he said despairingly.

'But, given that we will always have wars and will continue to have them . . .' Sarah raised her hand as Phil tried to interrupt '. . . and recognising that the human race should strive towards peace, and reasoned negotiation of disputes . . . And agreeing that that is the ultimate aim, and the best possible way of dealing with things . . . Nevertheless due to our own frailty, armed conflict does happen. So therefore I think it is probably preferable to have some basic code of conduct.' She smiled at him. 'End of lecture.'

Phil shook his head. 'By accepting a code of conduct you accept that negotiation doesn't work and you give up trying to make it work.'

'God, you are stubborn,' said Sarah. 'In one sense you are right. The peace process doesn't work in all situations. It's almost as though people *want* to fight. But, if you study modern trends, and as history progresses, I do think that many nations are accepting the futility of war. The situations where people are trying to achieve peaceful settlements are happening more and more. Look around the world, Phil,' she begged him. 'People *are* making the attempt. And *that's* what's important ultimately. People making the attempt.'

Phil chewed his lip. 'I suppose so,' he said at last.

'*And*,' said Sarah, pressing home her advantage. 'I am convinced that the Army has a very definite role as peace-keepers. So does my gran, and she lived through two world wars.'

Phil leaned forward and put his head in his hands. 'I dream about it,' he whispered. 'I've never experienced anything so horrific.'

Sarah nodded and moving closer to him she took one of his hands in her own. 'Me too,' she said.

They leaned against each other for a moment.

'And maybe I'm a moral coward in not facing up to the fact that the girl had to die.' Phil gave a huge ragged sigh. 'Because . . . part of me agrees that she *did* have to die. See . . . I know, that if it had been one of Ben's command tasks and I'd been in charge,' Phil waited a long moment before he spoke again. 'I'd have shot her.'

Sarah looked at him. His head was bent so low as to almost reach his knees. She couldn't see his face, but she knew that there were tears in his eyes. And as she watched Phil and listened to him speaking to her, she saw that David was wrong. It wasn't at all that Phil saw things in black and white. He saw all sides, could appreciate the other point of view. It was his deep sensitivity which made him so strung out, his ability to question his own beliefs. He recognised the ruthlessness within himself and was tortured by doubt.

She searched in her head for something to say to lighten his mood. She went close to him and nuzzled the side of his face. 'I don't know,' she said. 'Perhaps in battle conditions you wouldn't be quite such a mean machine.'

'Ben thinks I would. He has tried to persuade me to come on the selection weekend. He told me I was officer material. He thought I'd be pleased.' Phil wiped his face with his hands. 'I didn't know whether I found that more terrifying or depressing.'

'But you were a bit pleased,' said Sarah shrewdly, 'weren't you?'

Phil raised his head and looked at her. 'Smart kid,' he said.

'You must know that you performed well at the away day,' she went on. 'Your natural qualities of leadership came to the surface. It was the same with the command task, you could appreciate very quickly what had to be done.'

'What are you saying?' he asked her.

'That Ben is right,' she answered him. 'You have innate abilities which are compatible with soldiering.'

'But maybe soldiering isn't compatible with me . . . with my spirit.'

'Then if you believe that to be the case you must choose a different path. You have to be at one with yourself.'

'What about you?' said Phil. 'Do you think you'll follow it right through?'

Sarah thought for a long moment. 'Truthfully I don't know yet. I find the training and exercises thrilling and challenging, but I do realise that if I'm going to take it up full-time then there has to be more substance to it . . . I want to find out what else is involved, what it has to offer.'

She looked across the grass to where the rugby teams were assembling. Phil followed the direction of her eyes. 'I need to speak to David,' he said.

He looked at her as they stood up to walk towards the sports pavilion. 'What worries me I suppose, is the fear that being in the Army could brutalise someone . . .' he tailed off.

Sarah held his gaze. 'You mean by becoming a soldier I might lose my sensitivity?' she asked.

He nodded.

'It *is* something I've thought about,' she said seriously, 'whether joining the Army would mean I'd become less compassionate. So the best thing for me to do is to go on the selection weekend. After that I can make a decision. By then I'll have discovered more about the Army . . .' Sarah stopped and smiled at Phil, '. . . and more about myself.'